BOOK 3: Egypt to Crete

CW01507763

Dedication

The history of clay is long. The potters and artists are many. The spirit of clay ties together people of all cultures, all times and all places. Generation after generation, the people of the earth have been, and still are, all directly or indirectly connected through a clay experience.

This book is dedicated to all those unknown potters and artists that advanced the history of clay with discoveries, inventions and creations. Thank you all. It couldn't have been done it without you.

A NOVEL HISTORY OF CLAY

FOREWORD

I am a ceramic artist writing a novel about clay. I discovered the magic of clay when I was thirty. Now, fifty years later, as an artist and teacher, I wanted to sum up as much of my knowledge as is possible.

There are so many great "how to" and beautifully illustrated artists' biography books in the world that I thought I'd take a different approach.

I would write a book showing people and their lives actually experiencing clay–making discoveries and creating objects in their times and places–a book that was not only informative, but entertaining to read. That desire led to a historical novel format with characters and plots, real history and locations of events.

Clay and man have a long history together–over 30,000 years. I soon found the volume of information so vast that it was best to break it down into a series of more manageable units.

My conception for this series was to highlight each major discovery or technological advance in man's love affair with clay.

A NOVEL HISTORY OF CLAY

AMAZEdition 1

ISBN: 9798691133596

Copyright 2020, Paul Rideout

Published by Palul.com

A NOVEL HISTORY OF CLAY

BOOK 3:

Egypt to Crete -The Pursuit of Glazes

Paul PALUL Rideout

3

A NOVEL HISTORY OF CLAY

COVER PHOTO

Canopic Cat

A Ceramic Container by PALUL

A NOVEL HISTORY OF CLAY

BOOK 3

BOOK 3: Egypt to Crete

Because clay has such a long history with innovations thousands of years apart, each major discovery within its time period required a different set of characters and sub-plots. The resulting stories are strung together by one major thing–clay–both as a construction material and as fired historical objects that travel through time and space for generations and generations.

For a novel, questions surrounding each event had to be answered: Who's in power? What's happening? What was civilization like then? What was the geography of the locations where events take place? And even: What were the weather conditions there and then? I estimate for every hour of writing there are five hours of research.

Some technical things had to be reduced to our contemporary linguistics. Obviously, the many spoken languages had to be presented in a single language (English). For clarity, the various units of weights and measures used over time were consolidated into our current systems.

As for biographical information of characters, research on subjects before the 18th century is slim and questionable in accuracy. In order to develop plots I tried to get under the skin of characters, some real and some fictional, ad-libbing possible life experiences that could have happened in some way related to clay. Hence, personal events of characters are questionable but the histories of the times are real (as much as written history is true).

A NOVEL HISTORY OF CLAY

In this endeavor, I hope the reader will be both informed and entertained.

Good reading, my friends.   -Palul

BOOK 3

Egypt to Crete -The Pursuit of Glazes

2000 BC - The Eastern Mediterranean

Aaron and Nakht's Journey

9

A NOVEL HISTORY OF CLAY

List of Characters and Places

Aaron -protagonist
Mentuhotep II -Pharaoh
Neferu II -Mentuhotep II's sister and wife
El Kab -Aaron's home town
Ram Da -pottery shop owner in El Kab

Kluk -the pharaoh's ambassador
Thebes -capital city of Egypt during Mentuhotep II's reign
Kheti -pharaoh's treasurer
Alim -alchemist
Nakht -Aaron's good friend

Captain Sebek -ship's captain
Ugan -Captain Sebek's first mate
Katach -store owner in Taurus Mts
Niko -old chief
Nina -chief's granddaughter
Zah -chief's grandson

Zakros -East Crete coastal city, palace
Plagin Mt -Water source for Zakros, 900 ft high
Ahatt -Minoan Navy captain
Jon -Nakht's younger brother, Ahatt's first mate
Charn -harbor-master at Zakros

BOOK 3: Egypt to Crete

Ebu -old master potter on Crete
Amelia -Ebu's strong-willed assistant, bull leaper
Knossos -a capital city in Crete
Xantopos -Nakht's father at Knossos
Kar -Nakht's youngest brother

Khnum -potter's god, god that created man
Carii -Fellow potter at Ebu's
Xnos -A bull leaper
Cypro-Minoan -an ancient Mediterranean language
Britomartis -Minoan goddess of protection of sea and hunting

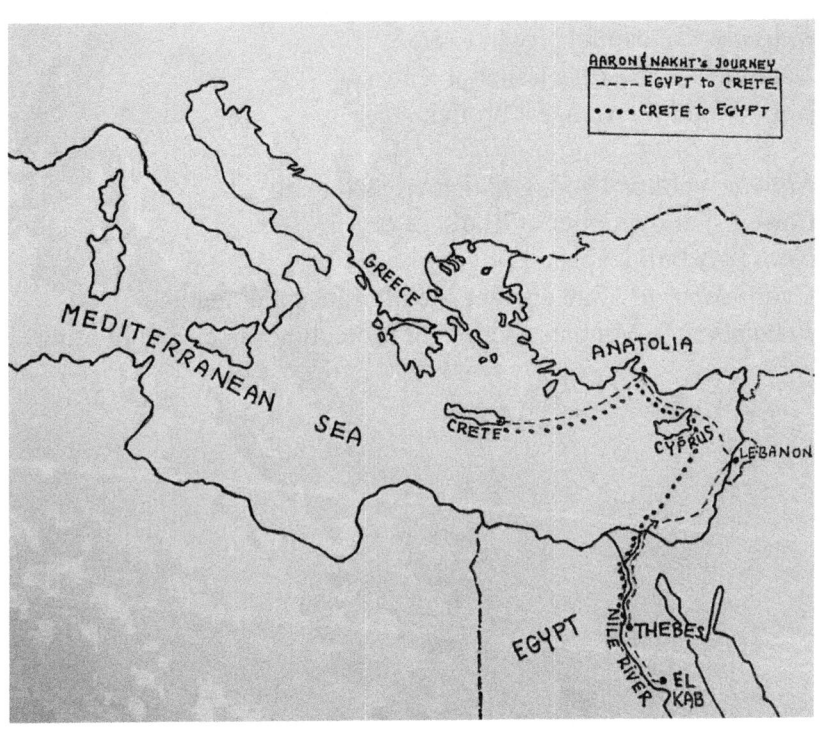

Aaron and Nakht's Journey

BOOK 3: Egypt to Crete

Middle Egypt 2000 BC

Aaron hoed thirty-five pounds of desert sand into his finely-woven basket. The tiny granules sparkled in the morning sun. He knelt, laid his hoe down and slung the basket over his tanned shoulders. He adjusted the pack and picking up his hoe, rose with some effort. The basket was heavy and he leaned forward for balance. The heavily-loaded teenager turned his back to the sun and using his hoe as a walking stick, began his hike home on calloused bare feet.

A mile ahead of him, to the west, the desert opened to a wide swath of fertile land that separated him from the Nile River. Behind him the hot desert shimmered dividing the sky from the desert in a rolling blur, preparing itself for the vicious onslaught of one-hundred-fifteen degree afternoon heat.

A vulture, flickering white against a clear blue sky, glided overhead in the direction of El Kab, a little town on the east bank of the Nile. Aaron's home was on the outskirts of El Kab at the edge of the Eastern Desert where the sun rose over pink and tan dunes.

The moving shadow of the gliding vulture passed a few feet across the sand in front of Aaron. He looked up.

"Wow," he exclaimed out loud to himself, "A white vulture! A sign from *Nekhbet*. The goddess signals good fortune!" He smiled inwardly and thought, *This will be a good day.*

The flood season had ended. A small canal, now a slow, lazy stream near Aaron's home reached a mile back to its source, the Nile.

***

The people of ancient Egypt recognized three seasons: flood, growth and harvest. Seasons were further divided into four months. Each year between May and August, high on the summits of Africa's Ethiopian Highlands, big cumulus clouds gather, dense, gray and wet. They open like giant shower-heads dropping monsoons that quickly gather into rivulets which flow swiftly down the slopes emptying into raging rivers. The huge deluge of waters empties into the Nile River which swells massively and flows from south to north carrying the precious liquid over 4000 miles through desert lands to the Mediterranean Sea. The southern area is called Upper Egypt as it is higher land. The country drops as the Nile flows north into the delta region where it fans out into a number of smaller channels that empty into the Mediterranean Sea. Being much lower in altitude, the region is called Lower Egypt.

Each year on the journey north the Nile overflows its banks on both sides for several miles inland. The annual floods deposit a rich black silt all along the river's edges which turns to a green swath of land in the growth season. So rich is this soil, that it is, and always has been, the life source of Egyptian civilizations.

***

Aaron knew of distributaries, man-made canals that worked their way from the Nile out to the edges of the desert. One such waterway passed close to his family's home. If he wanted, Aaron could climb into his little reed boat and pole all the way to the big river. The canals cut deep into the soil when the floods came.

Now a slow, lazy stream, a small canal, near Aaron's home reached three miles back to its source, the Nile. By each flood seasons' end, the waters shallowed and trickled in some places leaving grassy banks high above. In some places, thick clusters of papyrus reeds grew fifteen feet high on either side of the canals. Their denseness and feather-like crowns created shaded, green canyons for Aaron's little boat to pass through, a respite from the Egyptian heat.

Along the canal banks, frogs and snakes were plentiful. Egrets flew low over the reeds landing on long legs in muddy puddles. Occasionally a small crocodile basked in the black mud warmed by the Egyptian sun. Bigger crocs stayed closer to the Nile where maneuverability was easier and the game was larger.

A NOVEL HISTORY OF CLAY

The Nile has long been the road to other worlds. Along the shores for over 3000 years Egyptian towns and cities have appeared and disappeared. Each one had its palaces, shops, and tombs with hieroglyphics expounding the god-life of a pharaoh. In Egypt's *Intermediate Era (2200-2050 BC)* over a thousand years of ruins already dotted the shores.

***

Aaron's trip from his family's home to the potter's shop was easy during the growth and harvest seasons. However, poling against the inflowing waters of the flood season slowed his progress considerably. Some day, Aaron promised himself, he would pole on down into the Nile and drift in its currents all the way to the end. He had heard at the end there was a water so large you couldn't see the other shore.

East of his family's farm was endless desert, a source of income for the boy. Aaron helped support his parents and two younger brothers by selling desert sand to the local pottery. From his family's home the pottery lay on a high bank a mile and a half down the canal toward the Nile. The pottery had served the area so long that no one remembered when or how it began. The current owner, Ram Da, paid Aaron well saying his sand was the best they had ever used.

Having grown up on the desert's edge, Aaron knew of massive sand dunes a half mile from his home, dunes that were nothing but this fine sparkly sand. He felt rich in his knowledge.

16

BOOK 3: Egypt to Crete

An important part of Aaron's pay was an apprenticeship in the pottery shop. Pottery was one of those businesses in which the product could be easily broken, thus clay products were always in demand–in other words potters had steady work.

Industrious as he was, Aaron worked energetically all the time. His employer loved it and by the time he was 16, Aaron was familiar with the whole ceramic process. He had also learned just enough hieroglyphs to keep basic records of the business.

He liked the sculpting, but loved the mixing of materials. One could say he really understood the nuances of soils. So much so, that in his spare time, he began mixing different proportions of the same two materials together: clay and sand. He added water and rolled small test coils, numbering each. He used small clay bowls to measure out the different proportions. Keeping precise records of the sand to clay ratios, he used a charcoal stick to mark fire-hardened clay tablets with his test samples. The shop's potters fired the tests in their kilns along with their regular pots to bright yellow heat. Aaron diligently recorded the results with his simple hieroglyphs.

One mix of the sparkly sand and clay became shiny and bluish after firing. Not all sands caused the gloss, only his sparkly sand worked. And only a certain ratio of his sand to clay made the fired end product shiny blue. Too much sand and the test coil would fall apart. Too little and the product often cracked and looked dry and brown like the common potters' wares. Aaron memorized his ratio and formula for the glossy blue. He did not know it at the time but it would lead to an unforgetable adventure.

His fellow workers marveled about the new material and made blue beads, jewelry, and small trinkets out of this sticky mixture. Bigger objects fell apart from the lack of sufficient binding material. Soon the shinny little pieces spread into Lower Egypt. The blue, a turquoise blue, appealed to the aristocratic women, those who could afford to show off the latest fashions including jewelry.

The local pottery flourished and soon Aaron was making trips with the pottery owner to the Nile River. There they sold the blue beads, jewelry and little sculptures to a trader who transported them down the Nile to the larger towns and cities where he made profitable trades. The intense blue beads and jewelry soon became sought after by the upper classes. The demand grew and eventually reached the Pharaoh's court in Thebes.

***

Neferu II was the wife and sister of the Pharaoh, Mentuhotep II. The late morning light filtered through the window in her dressing room. Attendants scurried about beautifying her for the day's events.

"Have you seen the new blue jewelry?" asked her personal aid as she applied an iridescent greenish-purple kohl around Neferu's eyes.

BOOK 3: Egypt to Crete

Vanity is as old as man's history. In ancient Egypt both men and women wore copious amounts of makeup. The eye dressing, kohl, was especially popular with the wealthy. Grinding ores such as green malachite and galena (a form of lead!) with assorted oils produced the cosmetic. It was believed the makeup gave the wearer the protection of the gods Horus and Ra.

"Not only have I seen it, I have a scarab broach recently brought from somewhere south," answered the queen. "These blue-green objects are so beautiful, we must find out where they are coming from and get more."

She nodded to an attendant who brought the broach to her.

"Look how it shines in the light. The gold setting enhances the blue perfectly. I have shown it to the pharaoh's concubines. They are so envious. We must have more."

"Oh, yes!" agreed Neferu's attendant. Perhaps she too could acquire a small sample of the new blue jewels.

***

The queen's desires soon reached the pharaoh's ears. With the all-reaching power of the pharaoh, an ambassador soon arrived at the pottery in El Kab. Since the the pottery was small, the quantity of the little blue pieces was limited. Certainly the value increased by the laws of supply and demand: the fewer the pieces the higher the price.

"Who discovered this marvelous blue material?" the ambassador questioned the shop's owner.

One of our workers," answered Ram Da. "He figured out how to make the stuff from just clay and sand. He's a pretty clever fellow."

"How do you make it?" said the ambassador.

"Simple. Five parts sand to one part clay," relayed Ram Da. "After it dries we fire it in the kiln."

The ambassador returned to the Pharaoh and relayed the simple formula. The court alchemist and his potters immediately proceeded to mix the ratio. They were not used to mixing such a small amount of clay to sand but mixed it anyway. After firing, the pieces were a complete failure. After several attempts, the pieces that did hold together were dry and matte without any blue color. Had they been given the wrong formula? If so, the deceptive pottery shop would be punished.

***

The ambassador, along with two soldiers, returned to the pottery.

When questioned, a nervous Ram Da said, "It doesn't always work, sir."

"Why not?"

"We don't know."

"Surely the discoverer will know. Bring him to me," said the ambassador.

BOOK 3: Egypt to Crete

Ram Da found Aaron and brought him before the Pharaoh's representative. The Pharaoh's man was direct, a man who expected straight answers.

"We want more of the blue gloss ware. We tried your formula but it doesn't work. Can you tell us why?"

Aaron replied, "The sand must be my special sand. Ordinary sand doesn't work."

Aaron had also made the observation that the pieces located near the spy hole openings in the kiln turned out in the glossy blue, but other pieces of the same formula in other parts of the kiln glossed but failed to turn blue.

"I think it needs to be fired near an air port, too," he said.

The ambassador did not want to return with information that might not work. He would have failed in the eyes of the Pharaoh and could be severely punished, even executed for his failure. He decided to bring this young worker, Aaron, back to court to demonstrate to the court's potters and the Pharaoh how these blue treasures were made. If the boy failed, Aaron would be punished, not the ambassador.

"Have a ton of this special sand gathered," the ambassador said to Ram Da. "I will take it back along with your employee, Aaron, to the Pharaoh's pottery. There, this Aaron will show us how to create the blue gloss substance."

No one questions the Pharaoh or his men so the pottery had to

A NOVEL HISTORY OF CLAY

comply.

***

We know the basic formula for clay is:

$$2\ SiO_2 \cdot Al_2O_3 \cdot 2\ H_2O.$$

There are two types of water found in wet clay. The water that evaporates when drying clay pieces in the air is called <u>water of plasticity</u>. It's what makes the clay soft and moldable.

The second type of water is <u>chemically bound</u> to the clay as shown in its formula above. This water remains attached even when the clay has dried in 100 degree temperatures for days. Only extremely high heat can break the chemical bond.

The three basic ingredients for a glaze are silica, alumina, and a flux. The silica makes the glass. The alumina stiffens the glaze keeping the melted glass from running off the pot. And the flux melts the glaze. By varying the ratios of these three components (silica, alumina and flux) a glaze can be made to melt at specific temperatures. Whether a glaze is matte or glossy depends on the amount of alumina and fluxes present. With a lot of flux a glaze can be made to melt at very low temperatures.

So it is the flux that is added to the clay that lowers the temperature. What are some fluxes? Sodium and potassium are two of the most active fluxes. They are so active they are not found as pure elements but are found in compounds such as sodium carbonate, salt, and potassium carbonate. The heavy

22

BOOK 3: Egypt to Crete

metals such as lead and arsenic are also strong fluxes. Iron, copper, cobalt and manganese, although primarily used as coloring agents in glazes, also have strong fluxing properties.

So if you add a sufficient amount of these fluxing materials to clay you will lower the melting point. (By itself, silica melts at almost 3000 F; alumina about 3700 F. These are very high temperatures. In ancient days kiln temperatures did not reach more than 2100 F. A flux was vital to lower the temperature to obtain a glassy glaze.)

In chemistry-physics there is an event called a <u>eutectic point</u>. When two or more compounds are mixed in the proper ratio and heated, a eutectic point event occurs when the breakdown of the elements results in a lowering of the melting point that is less than either of the two individual compounds by themselves.

Thus, silica and alumina with their high melting points, can be radically lowered by merely adding other compounds–fluxes, such as sodium carbonate, lead or copper.

What happened with Aaron's sand has to do with its composition. Sand is the result of the breakdown of rocks. The type of rock determines what chemical elements are in the sand. Almost all sands have feldspars in them. Feldspar rocks are combinations of silica and alumina with various other elements. When used in glaze making, they contribute silica, alumina and fluxing elements. Given enough heat some feldspars are glazes by themselves.

A NOVEL HISTORY OF CLAY

Aaron's sand (a feldspar) had the property of an extremely high amount of sodium carbonate, a very strong fluxing agent.

Sodium carbonate (also commonly known as washing soda and soda ash) is water soluble (dissolves in water) and efflorescent; that is, it foams when wet. Because of this property, when the potters added water to Aaron's sand/clay mixture the dissolved sodium carbonate rose to the surface and effloresced. Upon drying it left a thin layer of sodium on the surface of the sculptured piece. When heated to a bright orange color (around 1700 F), the sodium, being a super powerful flux, melts the mix into a glossy surface.

The other part of this mix involves copper. The composition of Aaron's sand also included about 3% copper. Pure metallic copper is reddish. Copper oxide is blue-green (ever see a green penny?). When the sodium carbonate/copper/sand mix was added to the clay, the resulting pieces turned blue-green from the copper oxide wherever oxygen was present.

In wood-burning kilns there is little or no oxygen except near the spy holes where plenty of oxygen enters. Hence, only those oxygenated areas produced the desired blue-green color. The El Kab potters soon learned to leave lots of open holes in their kilns to get the beautiful blue effects which came to be known as *Egyptian paste.*

Egyptian paste is not considered a glaze. It is more of a low-fire clay body. If you broke a sculpture of Egyptian paste you would find the color not just on the surface like a glaze, but throughout the entire body of the figure.

It is a tribute to the scientific minds of the ancient Egyptians to recognize their many advances in the technologic fields of geology, chemistry, physics, astronomy, architecture and medicine to name a few.

***

Twenty 100 pound baskets of sand (which came to be known as "Aaron's sand") were rafted down the canal from the pottery to the waterfront of El Kab. From there it was loaded aboard the Ambassador's boat. Aaron rode in the boat with the ton of sand down the Nile River toward the pharaoh's capital city of Thebes. The large city drew citizens from up and down the Nile, both workers and shoppers.

Aaron would be a worker. He was both excited and nervous at the prospect.

***

The ambassador's reed boat, being an official vessel, floated smoothly, had a good-sized cargo hold and roofed cabins both fore and aft. A steersman handled a large rudder in the stern while oarsmen on each side of the center cargo-hold rowed. Since the boat was drifting downstream, only four rowers, two on each side, were necessary. When going up-river against the flow the full complement of ten rowers were employed.

Aaron and the ambassador stood on the bow watching a group of cormorants diving underwater and coming up with small fish in their saw-toothed beaks. The birds quickly turned their beaks skyward and with a shake let go allowing the fish to slide downward into their waiting gullets.

The ambassador turned and studied Aaron.

"Where are your sandals?" asked the ambassador. "And are those the only clothes you have?"

"I don't have sandals. My feet are tough from the desert. And what I wear is what I have on."

"You are going to a city, my young friend. People wear clean clothes and decent foot-ware. I cannot present you to the treasurer dressed like a slave. I have extra sandals and clothes in my cabin. Come with me and I will loan–no, give them to you."

Ambassador Kluk had taken a liking to the open-faced young man. With a little cleaning and dressing, he would make Aaron presentable to even the Pharaoh should the occasion miraculously arise.

"Thank you," said Aaron. "How long will it take to get to Thebes?"

"It will take three days. There are still a few stops on the way," said Kluk. "Wash and meet me in the Imperial Cabin and I will get your new clothes and sandals. You can sleep in the guest quarters during this trip."

BOOK 3: Egypt to Crete

The 50 mile trip on the slow-moving river from El Kab to Thebes passed dreamily by for Aaron. Slow rivers can have that effect–a smooth and steady rolling on.

Along the way villages appeared between stretches of farmland that grew large fields of flax. The flax was planted close together to encourage tall slender stocks which, when processed, were softened by pounding and then woven into linen clothing. Because of the hot weather most Egyptians wore only loin cloths or wraps made of linen. For those who could afford them, linen tunics were worn on more formal occasions.

Large crocodiles sunned along the shores between tall date palms. Occasionally the eyes and ears of hippopotamuses poked above the cooling water. The boat made a wide berth around these temperamental animals. They were easily annoyed and with their massive weight and huge mouths could easily sink a boat. Other animals such as boars, bears and even lions could occasionally be seen drinking at the water's edges. Flocks of white ibis' sat on branches of low trees surveying their river territories. A host of smaller birds flittered about the shore picking at insects and worms in the black mud.

The ever-present sun illuminated the landscape in dazzling light, glittering like mirrors off the low, slow waves of the Nile. The balmy nights on the river filled Aaron's ears with the intermittent sounds of frogs and night hawks.

Ambassador Kluk and the boat's crew treated the boy well,

offering him a fine beer with meals of fruits and breads. It was the first stage of Aaron's dream.

**

On the third afternoon they reached *Thebes*, the new capital city of Egypt. Pharaoh Mentuhotep II, on the advice of his treasurer, Kheti, had moved the old capital, *Inbu Hedj* (Memphis), to Thebes, a more central location.

The city boomed with riches. Six 80-foot obelisks pierced the skyline, white against blue. Between them, the Pharaoh's main palace reached three stories high with pillars on each floor holding lintels decorated with hieroglyphics and relief carvings depicting the gods and Mentuhotep II's deeds of valor. Throughout the palace, paintings, carved stone statues and hieroglyphics intimidated viewers with awe. Open court yards with pools and gardens dotted the complex. Even a zoo of exotic animals roamed and nested in a semi-forest of palms.

Immediately in front of the palace, spreading all the way out to the shore of the Nile, was the center of industry. This area housed the craftsmen. Along with a huge pottery complex which produced both functional wares and large intricate architectural elements and statues, a big warehouse stored the raw materials necessary for the creation of the arts. Aaron's sand would be tagged and stored here.

A large number of stone carvers as well as metal workers, jewelry people, weavers, woodworkers, entire kitchens with

BOOK 3: Egypt to Crete

cooks from all corners of Egypt, butchers and brewers, and even a school teaching hieroglyphics surrounded the palace. Physicians and scribes also dwelled in the immediate vicinity of the Pharaoh. Activity swarmed around Mentuhotep's palace. This area is where Aaron would be situated. From the lonely wilds of the desert's edge to a metropolis of busyness, Aaron's world did not just expand; it exploded.

Kluk directed Aaron to follow him to visit the treasurer, Kheti, in order to "administratively" log him in on the city register as a government employee.

"You will be housed in the potter's section. You will work under Alim, the alchemist. He will guide you in your duties. We will be pleased to see the results," said the treasurer. He then added in an authoritative and intimidating voice, "And I'm sure there will be positive results."

The country boy hoped the treasurer could not hear his knees knocking below his newly acquired tunic.

"Come with me," said Kluk and exited out the door.

They headed into a maze of buildings. Aaron thought he would be lost in this city. Streets went this way and that. There were big stone buildings and smaller wooden ones. People of all classes mixed together creating a cornucopia of sounds–yells, laughter, whistles, clattering, hammering and animals braying and screeching. Cooking fires and kilns generated a pale smoke that impregnated the air with a mix of the sweet smells of roasting meats and burning wood. A slight breeze from the river blew the oder of cooking spices into his nose and Aaron became hungry.

Kluk pointed to a group of large buildings. "Over there," he said. Aaron could see a thin white smoke from firing kilns rising over a wall that no doubt was the potter's district. They rounded a corner into a big courtyard where two of six kilns were firing. While workers stoked the kilns, other workers were unloading one kiln and still others were loading two more.

The aura of a busy industry saturated the area. There were pots and sculptures in stacks ready to be fired. Finished pieces were being checked for quality and packaged for transporting. Aaron could not believe how big it was. Compared to the pottery in El Kab this was astronomical. How could he find his way around here?

He stopped thinking about it and followed Kluk to a large building with a portico front. The portico, consisting of a flat roof supported by limestone columns at regular intervals, provided a shaded area where workers ate and gossiped during lunch breaks.

Standing in the portico, Aaron could see three large open entrances to three rooms. The rooms were large and illuminated with rays of light passing through doors and high windows. In the central area of each room he could see four enormous pillars holding up heavy limestone lintels arranged in an open square.

BOOK 3: Egypt to Crete

Thick palm tree beams spanned from the lintels to the side walls. Smaller beams criss-crossed the thick ones supporting layers of palm branches which, although Aaron could not see from looking up, supported a six to ten inch layer of adobe. A layer of bitumen (asphalt) covered with a coat of whitewash (calcium carbonate) sealed the roof.

Several feet above the square opening, an angular cupola overhung the roof allowing in light and air, cooling the room below like an air conditioner. Smoke from within the rooms also exited through the venting cupola. In addition, the overhang of the cupola protected the rooms below from infrequent rains.

As they walked in the shade of the portico, Kluk pointed out each room's activity.

"This one is mold-making. This one is for the new wheel work. The wheel design comes from an area in the middle east called Mesopotamia. We're still trying to figure out how to use them. Sati over there seems to work the wheels the best."

Kluk nodded to a muscular young man in a loincloth who squatted next to a wheel pushing it around with a pointed stick. Wet brown clay covered his hands and arms. Smudges of clay blotched his chest and more of the brown clay smeared his loincloth. A trickle of the wet clay had run down his legs and dried to a tan crust in the Thebes heat.

"How's it going, Sati?

"It's not easy, ambassador. The stick part's pretty tricky to master," said Sati. He reached up with one muddy hand and scratched his shaved head adding to the blotches already crusting there. "Sabu over there has designed a different way, using a slave in a pit beneath to turn the wheel. It seems to work ok, but you have to keep coordinated with the slave."

Aaron could see the slave's head bobbing up and down as he spun the wheel by rapidly pushing a cross of wood bars attached at the bottom of the wheel's shaft.

"Well, keep at it," Kluk encouraged.

The third room was further partitioned by seven foot walls into three cubicles. Each cubicle was about twenty feet square with one side fully open to the portico side of the room. A worker could look through the opening, across the portico hall and between the columns into the courtyard of kilns. The view gave a feeling of inclusiveness and excitement, a feeling that Aaron liked.

Inside the middle cubicle, Aaron could see rows of ceramic containers on wooden shelves that were attached to the cubicle walls from bottom to top. Each container had an identification mark, a hieroglyphic code of its contents. A big table occupied the center of the cubicle.

At the table an old man sat on a stool weighing a white powder into a bowl. He wore a white robe, low sandals and a wide, jeweled bracelet on his upper arm that flashed with the colors of more than one type of stone.

BOOK 3: Egypt to Crete

"This is Alim. He will be your overseer," said Kluk. The old man turned and scrutinized Aaron. His dark eyes looked up and then down. His bald head reflected a flash of light as he moved. Wrinkles spread out from his eyes and turned upward when he smiled.

"How old are you?" he asked.

"Eighteen," said Aaron.

"You know how to make the blue art?" he asked.

"Yes, sir," said Aaron.

"Good. We tried based on the formula we received, but no luck. Be here in the morning and we will figure it out." A small smile showed on Alim's creased face. The jewels in his bracelet flashed red and silver as he moved his arms.

"Well then," said Ambassador Kluk, "let's get you something to eat and a place to sleep. The potter's quarter is right around the corner. You start in the morning."

***

Aaron was given a small room in a dormitory next to the workshop. The room had a thick reed mattress, a wooden stool and a reed storage chest. A small window with a wide sill let in light. A dozen other employees resided in the dormitory.

Kluk said, "This is your room. Enjoy your stay. Work hard and you will do fine," and left.

33

Being left alone in the room awakened the shock of coming from the country to the densely populated city. So many people, so much activity, and yet he felt alone, awkward, confined and disoriented. *What is expected of me?* he thought. Since he was hungry he left his room to see if he could find something to eat.

***

"You look lost. You must be Aaron." A young man with curly, rust-colored hair approached Aaron. Most Egyptians shaved their heads, even the women. It seemed odd to see such thick orange hair. Aaron found out later his new friend had come from a land far to the north, a big island in the middle of the great sea. He had an accent when he spoke. He seemed to be Aaron's age and had an open smile. Aaron liked him right away.

"How did you know my name?" Aaron asked in surprise.

"Alim said you'd be the young guy who looked lost," replied the curly redhead. "My name is Nakht. Alim asked me to find you and get you settled into our system. My room is next to yours. You hungry?"

"Starved."

"Come with me. The cafeteria is on the end of the building. It can get pretty smokey. They're always baking bread. You like beer? They have a great honey beer."

Aaron followed Nakht down a hall into the dormitory's dining room. A buzz of clinking plates and cooking utensils mixed with the sounds of conversations which frequently broke into laughter. The smells of fresh bread caused Aaron's mouth to water.

Nakht explained the dining routine and soon they were sitting at a table with breads, fruits and large mugs of beer.

Aaron admired the mugs. They held a half quart of the brew and had solid handles. Most everyone drank beer since the water was often dirty and, depending on the circumstances, full of bacteria (although micro-organisms were unheard of in ancient Egypt). The alcohol content "purified" the beer making it safer to drink. Because of a minimum of filtering the people drank through straws to avoid the surface debris. Wine was also made in Egypt, but it was expensive, a drink for the wealthy.

The curly haired Nakht described the city in his odd accent tossing in tidbits of information about various prominent citizens. The city's main focus was to support Pharaoh Mentuhotep II. He, like all pharaohs, was considered a god in human form. The health and happiness of Pharaoh Mentuhotep II determined the health and happiness of the people. Thus, all the people willingly worked for Mentuhotep II–even the slaves.

Although much labor involved preparation of a tomb for the Pharaoh's rebirth into the next world, the overall process had the effect of great progress in a multitude of the arts and sciences. The pottery workshops were no exception. The effects of heat on materials fell within the scope of the alchemists who worked closely with the potters and metal workers. The functional items of clay vessels and bronze weapons became more refined with time. The offshoot of the finer works, such as jewelry and detailed casting of items, inspired (with the approval of the Pharaoh, of course,) the experimentation with new materials. Aaron's sand, unlike regular desert sand, would become more than little blue sculptures.

***

In the morning Aaron entered Alim's workshop with Nakht. The old man had just arrived. Two additional apprentices, Benipe and Oni, made a total of five. A servant brought five cups of a hot tea-like beverage and set them on the central table. Alim and his workers each took a cup. Aaron took a sip. It tasted sweet and of peppermint. He looked about waiting to be told what to do for his first day.

Benipe and Oni had worked with the alchemist for many years and were advanced students of Alim. They could work independently and knew the procedures well. As soon as they finished their tea, Benipe, Oni and Nakht went to the shelves and began their daily routines cataloging and weighing materials from the storage jars. Alim had assigned them duties and projects. They would take charge when Alim could no longer work.

The Pharaoh's alchemists were highly respected. Most people considered them to be magicians. What it took to be an alchemist was, first of all, a sense of order. One also had to be a detailed observer and diligent recorder of those observations. The other, and perhaps the most important, characteristic of an alchemist was that of curiosity: *What will happen if I do this?*

In the alchemist's workshop three servant-slaves took care of the mundane things such as procuring food, water and supplies as well as washing and emptying waste containers. The servants also acted as messengers when needed. Clay slabs, etched with hieroglyphics, were used to convey information around the city.

The apprentices did much of the labor of weighing and labeling the materials, most of which was obtained from the adjoining storage warehouse. This big area housed Aaron's 20 baskets of sand along with an assortment of other materials such as clays and sand from different sites. A wide door opened to the outside through which dock workers delivered materials that arrived from outside the city limits. Most materials came by boat.

Two scribes stationed in the storage warehouse kept detailed records of incoming and outgoing materials. The clay and sand used in the multitude of ceramic objects occupied the largest space, an entire half of the room. Originally firewood for the kilns had filled a large section, but the dusty debris from the bark and twigs often contaminated the other materials. Now the fuel was separately and more efficiently stored under a roofed building next to the large kilns in the courtyard. Besides the wood, reeds and dried animal dung supplemented the fuel supply.

After assigning the other apprentices their duties, Alim motioned to Aaron.

"Usually we start apprentices with the more routine jobs, but you have been brought to us for a specific purpose. The Pharaoh–actually his wives and concubines–," Alim winked at his little aside, "they are enchanted with the blue gloss substance that your old pottery creates. We were given a formula but it does not work. I think you will be able to help us."

Aaron nodded. *How could such a massive and rich workshop not be able to create the blue pieces? It's so simple.* Aaron, the naive country boy, did not recognize his own brilliance. In every culture there are those whose curiosity, whose quest for knowledge, exceeds their own self esteem. Humility is a natural condition of the naive.

"I will be pleased to help, sir," he replied.

"You may call me Alim," said the old man. "Can you read?"

"A little," replied Aaron. "I know numbers."

"That's important. If you are interested in alchemy I will send you to the hieroglyphics school with Nakht. He is learning too. Do you want to go to school?"

Aaron could not believe his good fortune–a hieroglyphics school–an alchemist–what a wonderful place to work!

"Yes!" he exclaimed.

BOOK 3: Egypt to Crete

"Great. School is every other morning. Nakht will take you with him tomorrow morning. Now let's get to work.

Alim showed Aaron where supplies were kept. How to obtain the different materials and told him to be certain to check in and out with the scribes. He showed Aaron where different sizes of measuring bowls were located. He explained how a device called "scales" worked.

"The scales are more accurate than bowls or cups," said Alim. "The scales measure weight. The bowls measure volume. The scales can precisely measure small amounts of material. The bowls can be off quite a bit depending on if the material is packed in tight or loose. And most importantly, scales work with small quantities. Often we have little material to experiment with."

"Where do the materials come from? asked Aaron.

"They are brought to us from all around. Some ores from across the sea to the east (the Sinai Peninsula). Some from the coasts of East Asia. And a lot comes from your area in our own Upper Egypt."

"You mean they're imbedded in the rocks?"

"That's right. When a good vein of ore is discovered miners dig out the rocks, smash them up and ship them in crates to us. It's a hard hot job. I have been to a few mines. I would not like to be a miner, but, as an alchemist, I depend on the miners. I really appreciate them."

A NOVEL HISTORY OF CLAY

"It must be fun to explore for these rocks. I have seen rocks like that one in outcrops in the hills far into the desert near my home." Aaron pointed to a fist-sized rock on a shelf. The shiny gray rock had clusters of white sheaf-like crystals protruding from the sides."

"Really!" exclaimed Alim. "That's what we get tin from."

"I've seen some of that one too." Aaron pointed to greenish rock. This one had a rich turquoise vein running through it."

"That's copper ore," said Alim, becoming more impressed with his new apprentice.

"How do you separate the metal from the rocks? It must be difficult."

"A good question my young friend. After the ore has been mined and delivered, we first smelt it by putting it in a kiln and heating it. See that smaller kiln in the corner of the yard? We call that our blast furnace 'cause we blast air into it with bellows when it gets yellow hot. We use charcoal that we get from burning wood without air, or at least very little air, as a fuel to get the kiln really hot. As it gets hotter and hotter, the ore turns to a yellow-white color. Apparently the metal ores melt at lower temperatures than the rocks because the metal drips out in tiny droplets which fall into our collection plates beneath. That's how we separate the pure metals from the ore. Amazing, isn't it? I wish I could say I invented the system, but it seems to have been used for many years in old Mesopotamia before arriving here.

BOOK 3: Egypt to Crete

Our Nakht has seen these blast furnaces in other parts of the world and has been quite helpful in improving our processes."

Alim went to a shelf and brought down two lidded bowls. Aaron recognized one hieroglyph for copper. The other bowl had a symbol he could not read.

"I see you recognize copper," Alim said. "The other sign is for cobalt. We only have a small amount but it's a powerful blue. If we had more the Pharaoh would be happy. This came from far up the Nile, deep in the middle of Africa. It's source is a thousand miles from here. Explorers have been sent out to find more, but so far, little luck. When they do find it in large quantities it'll be more valuable than gold. Until then, you are here to create the bright blue."

Aaron quickly memorized the cobalt hieroglyph. Looking at more labels he recognized symbols on two more lidded pots, both had the sign for iron, but one had an extra squiggly line under it. Although iron had not been completely smelted and refined yet, the substances were of interest to Alim. It would be several hundred years before the Bronze Age would fade into the Age of Iron.

"Do these pots contain the same iron?" Aaron asked.

"No," said Alim pleased to see Aaron's observation. "The two irons are different in color. See." He opened the lids. Aaron looked inside. Each jar held a gravel of crushed rocks. One looked rusty red, the other gravel was almost black. "There is another substance that I think is also iron." Alim took down another jar and opened it. It was more powdery in texture and a yellow ochre in color."

It is true that iron comes in different forms. There is ferrous, ferric, ochre and iron pyrite.

"They're all difficult to get," continued Alim. "We crush and grind them, but because they are not as pure, they come out in speckles. Potters use the coarse granules to obtain various speckles of browns, from tans to almost black. What you get when fired depends not just on the kind, but also the quantity and the firing conditions. Also, what other materials the iron is mixed with matters."

Alim motioned to the servant-slaves. "Go the the storeroom and ask the scribes to give you one basket of Aaron's sand. Then get a basket of white clay and a basket of brown clay.

The servants soon arrived with the three baskets.

"Grind them up and give us a bowl of each," the alchemist dictated.

The servants knew the routine. Using thick ceramic bowls as mortars, bowls that curved smoothly so there was no break between the bottom and sides (as if they were all bottom and no sides) the servants began to grind the three materials separately using large rounded pestles.

The alchemists (and potters) always had their materials ground to a very fine powder (at least to what we'd call 100 mesh). The finer powders have a greater surface area and therefore melt together easier. Grinding also makes the powder more uniform from batch to batch.

"Do you need any other materials? Alim asked.

Aaron shook his head.

"No. Ok, what ratio do we mix?" said Alim as if he were the student.

Aaron, having memorized his formula, immediately responded: "five parts sand to one part clay."

Showing Aaron how to use the scales, Alim weighed out the sand.

"Which clay?" asked Alim.

"Your clay is different than the clay we had at home. Let's make two batches so we can see if there is a difference between the white and brown clays."

"Good idea." Alim liked Aaron's thoughtful approach. He, himself, would have suggested two batches as well.

"We need a little water," said Aaron.

Immediately a servant brought him a jug of water. The two batches were small in quantity so Aaron added just enough to make three samples of each batch into a thick and sticky paste. These they formed into tiny handleless cups. There were six test cups all together.

Alim had tried this before, but not with Aaron's sand. It was a simple mix. However, no matter what ratio he had tried, and he had tried many, the best he got was a slightly shiny, matte brown.

"They must dry 'til there is a white powder on the surface," said Aaron. "It's best to dry the pieces on some fired clay tablets so no one touches or smudges the surface. We just load both the tablet and sculpture into the kiln as one. It'll take a day or so to dry. If the powder is brushed off, it won't work."

This was a new concept for the old alchemist. *A white powder on the surface. Don't brush it off. If this works, this boy–this young man–will be a great asset.* The old excitement of his early days of discoveries flooded Alim's mind and he became excited.

***

By the next day the Egyptian heat had dried the little test cups. The surfaces had a lumpy coating of a white powder.

Alim modestly announced, "We have our own test kilns in the laboratory." (That's what Alim's workspace actually was–a laboratory.)

Aaron examined one of the small kilns. It actually was cute, although that was not the term a potter would use. The kiln's ware chamber held about one cubic foot of space. The firing box beneath was almost the same size. The chimney opening seemed

BOOK 3: Egypt to Crete

small and the construction was tight. A loose brick was used as a damper to cover the chimney to control the heat flow. Aside from a small spy-hole in the door, not much additional air could enter. It was a tight kiln.

Aaron would have liked more air to enter, but was afraid to say so. After all, this old man was a master. His kilns would be perfect.

They loaded four test cups, two using each clay body, into the little kiln. A small fire flamed in the fire box. As the kiln slowly heated, more fuel sent a flame through the chamber and a smooth, six inch yellow flame appeared out the chimney. The little kiln would fire fast. Anticipation filled the air.

Aaron, having experience, was concerned there was not enough free air in the kiln to make the pieces blue. He nervously looked about. There in the corner he saw an old test kiln. The bricks were loose and obviously not tight from having been used so much–a leaky kiln. He went over to the kiln and found he could actually pull out a brick or two in the side.

"Alim, do you mind if we fire these last two tests in this kiln?" he asked.

"Why would you want to use an old falling-apart kiln when you can use this new one?" replied Alim.

"It wouldn't hurt, would it? We do have these extra tests."

"Go ahead, my young friend," said Alim somewhat amused.

45

Aaron slid the remaining two tests into the old kiln and sealed the door. With a little torch of twigs, he lit a fire in the old kiln's firebox. As he added more wood, the yellow chimney flame climbed out only an inch. In an hour the yellow flam flickered six inches out. Aaron pulled out a side brick leaving a hole in the reddening kiln. He left the brick out. The flame in the chimney increased in size, but turned blue.

Alim and the servants watched Aaron in amusement. *He likes to play with fire. An interesting young man.*

By late afternoon both kilns were glowing orange-yellow inside. The fires died and the potter-alchemists finished for the day. They looked forward to the kiln opening in the morning.

***

Morning came and Alim and his apprentices gathered around the test kiln anticipating the results. *Would this boy from the south succeed where they had not?*

They removed the bricks covering the door to the still warm kiln. When they looked inside four shiny brown test pieces lay on the shelfs. Alim and his worker's faces looked disappointed. Even though the pieces had glossed nicely they had failed to turn blue. Close inspection showed a difference between the two clay bodies. The white clay was a much lighter brown. The darker clay body produced a shinier gloss but was a dark brown. It was attractive, but not blue.

"Too bad," said Alim. "Where do we go from here? I assume the tests in the other old kiln are the same. Open it up."

The disappointed group stood around the old kiln while Aaron removed the door bricks. When the bricks were piled aside and the group looked in, the astounded potters let up a cry of wonder. Smiles broke out and exclamations filled the room.

There on the brick shelf were two bright blue, glossy test pieces. Aaron had done it. He had the magic.

"My word," said Alim. "What did you do? How could you get the process to work in this old broken kiln and not in the new one?"

"To get the blue product, you need the blue flame," said Aaron. "You get the blue flame by letting more air (oxygen) into the kiln."

"And I thought you were playing, Aaron," said Alim. "Indeed, we have acquired the right person for our laboratory. Let's make some more pieces, fine jewelry for the Pharaoh's wife–for his concubines–for all the rich ladies!"

His enthusiasm was that of a youth. "Bring us some beer." The servant-slaves returned quickly with large jugs of warm beer and drank along with Alim and his apprentices. It was a memorable event.

The riddle of Egyptian paste had been solved and after fine tuning the procedure, the operation moved from Alim's lab to the production room next door. The Egyptian women (and thus the

A NOVEL HISTORY OF CLAY

Pharaoh) were thrilled with the new turquoise-blue jewelry.

***

In summery, Egyptian paste is an inorganic substance containing mostly silica (glass-maker) and soluble alkaline salts (fluxes) such as soda ash, sodium bicarbonate and potassium carbonate.

Although not necessary, a small amount of clay is often added to make it sticky and hold together when sculpting. Because of the lack of, or limited clay in the body, it is not good for large sculptures but can be molded or pressed into small compact shapes such as beads and figurines.

When air drying, the soluble salts (from Aaron's sand) migrate to the sculpture's surface leaving a powdery, white film. Firing the piece (oxidation at 1600-1900°F) causes the film to melt forming a bright, glazed surface over a highly vitrified body.

To get various colors, stains or oxides are mixed into the body. The main colorants are copper, cobalt, manganese, ochre and rutile. Further, mixtures of these colorants provide a greater range of colors.

One could say Egyptian paste is a cross between a glaze and clay body.

***

BOOK 3: Egypt to Crete

When Nakht was 13 he became a ship's cabin boy serving on a large trading vessel whose home base was the city of Knossos on Crete, an island in the middle of the Mediterranean. The ship picked up goods in one port and traded them for a profit in another. By the time Nakht was 16 he had visited coastal towns and cities all along the Eastern Mediterranean.

The captain was a shrewd trader and quite successful, but had a mean streak that occasionally resulted in beating his cabin boys.

Nakht had signed on to the trader's ship in Crete to "see the world." His earlier life, the son of a successful merchant in Crete, had given him a sense of security and self confidence–all would be well. However, he wanted to explore the world around him, and more so, to escape his father's limited ideas for his son's future. Hence, he had joined the crew of the trading ship and left Crete. His father was disappointed but he did have other sons who he would cultivate to carry on his business.

When the ship landed in the port of *Rhacotis* (Alexandria) in the Nile Delta carrying a large variety of goods, including fine Cretan pottery and exquisite gold and silver jewelry, wines, ores, lumber and linens, Nakht, having had enough of his captain's nasty temper, jumped ship. Jumping ship without thought of the consequences took a leap of faith (or naivety). The youthful Nakht soon disappeared into the busy port city. While wandering about he stumbled upon a shop that specialized in mineral ores.

Nakht had a gift for languages. He was a natural linguist, that is, he could easily pick up a foreign language wherever he went. When the ore shop's owner discovered Nakht's talent for languages he thought Nakht could become a good connection with the foreign speaking clients and offered him a position in the mineral shop. Needing money, Nakht eagerly accepted.

After a year at the mineral shop, the owner sent him into the Nubia region of Upper Egypt where the major deposits of ore were found. He was to locate new sources and ship them back to the business in the delta of Lower Egypt. It was there in southern Africa that he first became acquainted cobalt, an element that when used in glazes turns the glaze a deep blue.

On his return north, he stopped in Thebes. When he arrived in Thebes, he was 18 and spoke several dialects of Egyptian fluently. All was well until, with hormones raging, he discovered an attractive young Theban. So enamored was he that he quit his job and began to court her. When her father, a staunch local businessman, found the curly-haired redhead had no job, he forced his daughter to end the relationship. The girl's father found a good "local" man to marry her off to. She was not happy, but could not refuse her father's wishes. Nakht, at age 18, was devastated.

Because of his knowledge of ores Nakht eventually found work in Alim's laboratory. He was now 20 and comfortable in Thebes although his lost love left him a wary feeling about relationships.

When interviewed by Alim, it did not take the old alchemist long to recognize Nakht's potential. Besides the lust for knowledge, the young foreigner also possessed facts about other lands, lands where new materials might exist and thus new wonders might be revealed with laboratory methods.

So far, with the exception of his lost love, all was going well for Nakht. His time in Egypt had been a great learning experience, especially with the metal crafts, the substances of the earth that when heated to yellow-white heat would melt. The hot liquid metals could be poured into ceramic molds and all manner of things created.

While in Alim's service, Nakht managed to import a variety of rocks containing metal ores to experiment with. He worked with small batches of the rock ores, melting them in Alim's test kilns by using the available charcoal as a fuel and increasing the temperatures by using the skin-covered bellows that, when squeezed, blasted air into the fire with ferocious violence. As the ore heated to its melting point, it would drip out in little beads that he collected in small crucibles placed strategically beneath the mineral containing rocks. Once the metal was separated from its rock matrix into the little crucibles it was pure.

The separated metals could then be reheated at lower temperatures and poured into molds to create jewelry and other small items. Larger smelters already existed that manufactured weapons, chariot parts and the like out of bronze alloys.

With Alim's approval the curly redhead used more exotic rock

51

conglomerates seeking to find yet undiscovered metals. If tin and copper made bronze, why could there not be other combinations of substances refined from the earth that could make yet more marvelous things? This inquiring mind was what drove Nakht to Alim's laboratory.

Aaron, on the other hand, was a keen observer, a quick learner and kept excellent records. Having grown up at the desert's edge he could differentiate the nuances of sands and rocks. By observation of the shapes of rock formations, colors, and relative locations he could predict where the most likely areas would be to explore for new materials. Alim was pleased with both young men.

***

After several months in the lab, Aaron had produced a semi-gloss material from fine silica sand, crushed limestone, and small amounts of Aaron's sand. There was no clay added. The ground up mix of powder, when fired in a crucible to bright orange heat sintered and upon cooling became a semi-gloss, or a matte, hard substance. The tiny amount of copper in Aaron's sand had been so diluted in the mix that there was no color, just a transparent satin coating with quite a bit of crackle in it.

Nakht suggested they form the dry mix with a little water, shape it and fire it. Without clay as a binder it was difficult holding together so the mix was pressed into small ceramic molds, little statue molds that were used with the Egyptian paste forms. The results were smooth, but porous and a bit bland, lacking any color other than a pale dirt brown.

"Add a little of this," said Alim handing Aaron a jar of copper powder.

Aaron measured out several different amounts of the copper and recorded the amounts. He mixed together the correct proportions of silica, sand and Aaron's sand, measured out several small bowls worth and added separate quantities of copper to each. Everything was recorded by etching into thin clay slabs.

After pressing the mixtures into small forms, the pieces were placed in the test kiln to fire. The test kiln now had removable bricks which could be used as spy holes and to add, if desired, more air into the kiln. Aaron wrote down everything they did. His hieroglyphic class was proving to be a great aid. He could now pass on information to Alim and the apprentices easily.

The results of adding copper turned all the test pieces blue-green. The percentages of copper made a big difference. 1% and 2% barely turned green, 3% a light green-blue, 4% to 6% a medium green-blue, 7% to 8% a nice dark green, and more than 9% became a metallic black. There was a clear-cut ratio; the more copper the darker the result. From this point on, various additional colorants, both mineral and plant derivatives, were added to the new mix which came to be known as *Egyptian faience.*

Egyptian faiences have little or no clays in their formula and thus cannot be called clay bodies. The makeup of faiences resembles glazes, but are not applied as liquids like glazes. They do not melt like a glaze, but are more of a sintered-silica ceramic.

Egyptian faience's resistance to holding together in the raw state led to applying it over the surfaces of bisque-fired sculptures and then firing to completion. A particularly effective technique was to carve lines and textures into the sculpture and rub the faience mix into the crevices. The results of the heating produced strong rich colors in the crevices and softer colors on the surfaces.

It should be noted here that "Egyptian faience" is not the same as "faience" is used today. Sometime, before the ninth century in the Middle East, the process of putting a lead based glaze over an already fired tin-based white glaze became called faience. Tin is used as a whitener and to make a glaze opaque. In faience, it's like the tin glaze is the background and the lead glaze is the drawing on the surface or the foreground.

Because lead melts at such a low temperature (621.5°F), it became an ideal flux for low fire glazes and a solution for the fact that most European and Middle Eastern kilns could not reach the high temperatures needed for porcelain as was happening in China.

In the seventeenth century, European pottery collectors began using the term "Faience" to describe this lead-on-tin style of

BOOK 3: Egypt to Crete

pottery taking the name from the Faenza region of Italy where it was mass-produced. It was radically different from the old Egyptian faience.

***

The Pharaoh's production shops produced lots of small figurines called *shabtis* using the faience method. These were included with the dead in their tombs. They were, like slaves, believed to carry out tasks for the deceased in the underworld. However, it was necessary for the deceased's name to be inscribed on the base of each with clear instructions to send the *shabtis* into action. Such was one of the many details of death and rebirth for the people of ancient Egypt that kept the potters busy.

***

Shortly after the creation of (Egyptian) faience, Alim checked his stock of raw materials. There were two kinds, those raw materials such as the ores, rocks with the desired substances bound inside that had to be extracted by smelting, and pure specimens that did not have to be smelted. In both cases the ultimate materials were those that had been pulverized and were ready to be experimented with.

Although the pure materials were easier (no smelting necessary), the ores held a potential that the alchemist could learn the most from–the unknown, the undiscovered miracle substances. Alim wanted more. If he could turn rocks into gold, silver and precious gems, the Pharaoh would be pleased. Everyone, including Alim, knew that when the Pharaoh, the incarnation of a god, was pleased, all peoples would benefit.

It was in the philosophy of pleasing the all-powerful pharaoh that Alim pursued his profession. With the alchemist's successes and future promises of more riches, Mentuhotep II continued to supply Alim with financial support for the pursuit of alchemy.

Alim concluded his supplies were running low. He needed more. Rather than wait for whatever traders managed to deliver to Thebes, Alim took a more proactive position. He could send people out to find and discover more of the remarkable wonders of the earth. However, those he sent should know what they were looking for. Someone with knowledge. Someone with good observation skills. Someone who could understand and trade with foreign cultures.

Aaron had knowledge and good observation skills. He knew what to look for and where to look. But his knowledge was limited to Egypt, actually Upper Egypt.

Nakht had a more worldly view. He could speak in a myriad of tongues. He also knew how to trade, how to communicate with foreign people, how foreign cultures differed. Nakht seemed to fit in wherever he went.

With those thoughts in mind, Alim made a decision. Both Aaron and Nakht, together, would be sent to find new materials, Aaron could locate and confirm the materials. Nakht could negotiate and manage the shipping and delivery systems. Together they would make a good team.

Alim would miss these young men, but the rewards, the potential of them finding and delivering marvelous things was there. He would like to go himself, but at age 70 his energy had declined. Perhaps he should retire. Benipe and Oni could take over, but what fun would that be. Alchemy, the pursuit of knowledge, lived inside old Alim. He would be happy to die in his laboratory. He would sent his "boys" off to distant lands, to see new sights, to harvest the soils of the earth. They would be his vicarious self. When they returned there would be glory upon glories.

Alim made the announcement at the close of the flood season. The waters were still high. Ships could travel from Thebes downriver to Memphis and then through the diverse waters of the Delta into the Mediterranean. From there his two young apprentices would travel east along the coasts of Asia Minor and when Aaron saw what could be a fruitful location, a location of great rock formations, he could order the ship to find the nearest port. He and Nakht would then explore the area and, with the will of the gods, find a treasure of new materials to ship back to Thebes. Alim imagined himself making the journey and sighed. *My boys will be my legacy. They will carry on. They will find god's ultimate treasure.*

Upon hearing Alim's proposal, Aaron and Nakht looked at each other in disbelief. Aaron would see the world. Nakht would continue on to new places. They were both happy and excited.

Plans were laid. Supplies were gathered. Instructions were passed on to both young men. Alim estimated they would be gone a year. He would remain and carry on his research. He would wait. He would be ready to investigate the new materials, develop new sciences. He could depend on these two young men.

The Pharaoh approved. Anything to elevate his status was to be pursued. He assigned a ship with an experienced captain and crew, gave the captain instructions to go wherever the young men requested and to land wherever they wanted, even if there was no port. If a rich vein of treasure was found, they would build a port.

The captain met with Alim and the two young explorers in Alim's laboratory. His boat, Captain Sebek said, would follow the Pharaoh's commands. The two young men could pursue their goals. He and his boat would be at their disposal. Captain Sebek would guide the ship to and from ports, collecting and storing the expected treasures for the Pharaoh.

Before leaving, the ship's big holds were filled with millet, barley and wheat from the abundant grain harvest. Along with Egypt's renowned grains, finely worked jewelry was also loaded aboard for trading as necessary.

Also on board was a large, sleek gray cat, a respected mouser. Almost all large ships carried a cat or two. Reed ships, especially those carrying grain, attracted rats and occasionally a venomous

BOOK 3: Egypt to Crete

snake. Egyptians revered the cats as having magical powers as well as their more practical value of keeping snake and rodent populations restrained. Sailors highly valued their feline crewmates and many would not sail on a ship without at least one cat.

Hearing of Nakht's sailing history and that he could speak several languages gave a sense of confidence to Sebek. Three years on the water, even as a cabin boy, assured Sebek that this young man knew the water. He would not get seasick. The other fellow–well, Sebek would wait and see.

The Nile flowed high and smoothly northward. Soon Sebek's ship was cruising down the center of the Nile with only two oarsmen and a steersman necessary. The ship was similar to the ship that had taken Aaron to Thebes, but much bigger. Aaron and Nakht shared a large cabin room. The Captain said they would be able to classify and store as much as they could fit in the room. Memphis, the former capital of Egypt, would be reached in four days if the river continued at its current flow rate. They would drift day and night. Sailors liked the nights since they were cooler and quieter. Like most sailors, they drank a lot of beer and were constantly pissing over the side.

The trip would take them almost 500 miles north. They would dock in Memphis for a few days to resupply. Then they would travel into the Mediterranean and up the coast. Aaron (and the gods) would pilot from there. Hopes were high.

***

A NOVEL HISTORY OF CLAY

The former capital city of Memphis appeared on the horizon.

The boat docked, tying up at a long pier. Leaving two sailors to watch over the ship, the rest went ashore. Sebek and his sailors focused on negotiating for food and lodgings in the big city.

Because the capital had been moved to Thebes many years ago, the Memphis inhabitants still retained hostile feelings over their of loss of status. Sebek suggested the crew not mention they were from Thebes to avoid unpleasant confrontations.

The port authorities at Memphis, having been appointed by Mentuhotep II, were a different matter. Sebek had only to flash the Pharaoh's ring and the port bureaucracy went to work. Orders fanned out into Memphis and soon the necessary supplies began to appear on the docks. Carts and wagons appeared and resupplied the vessel with additional grains, dried meats, beer, and water for a long voyage.

On the third day the ship set sail again. When the boat entered the basin of the Lower Nile, the river forked into multiple branches. Sebek repeatedly selected the major forks to the right. He said they could save a day's travel that way.

They entered an ultramarine blue Mediterranean Sea. Sails were hoisted and with a steady breeze the adventurers left Egypt behind.

In two days West Asia's bountiful hills and mountains appeared. Aaron began to evaluate the various landscapes for formations that would indicate where to search for the desired metal ores.

BOOK 3: Egypt to Crete

Being in charge of choosing directions made Aaron nervous, even though Alim had given him a pep talk before leaving.

"You have good instincts." Alim had assured him. "The land can fool you. Don't be discouraged. And when you make a mistake, learn from it. I envy your journey. Follow your instincts, Aaron."

Nakht also had advice: "Look and enjoy. When you see something you like, we'll head that way. Remember we're explorers. Rarely does an explorer know where he's going. That's why they're called explorers."

Captain Sebek understood the youth's dilemma from the captain's point of view. Aaron was green, a rookie. When asked, Sebek gave advice and sometimes he would hint about directions. However, Aaron needed to get the feeling of being in charge. The responsibility of keeping the ship from being wrecked weighed on the captain's shoulders. Aaron needed only to watch the land along the coast. Sebek's role became that of protector of the ship and a guardian. Aaron felt comforted in that respect and frequently asked questions about traveling to both the captain and Nakht. The country boy seemed to adjust to the sea routine as well as any one could expect.

From the boat Aaron looked for mountains cut by a river. The river would tear away banks and expose the earth's undergarments. The mountain ranges to the east showed purple in the distance–too far away. He sought a range that could be

61

more easily accessed. A wide river emptying into the Mediterranean with a town dock would be best. Nakht could then talk to the locals for information and if plausible be guided along the river into the hills where prospecting seemed favorable. It seemed like gambling, but the captain and Nakht said it was the best way. Aaron agreed, even though another search method he employed was to look for outcroppings in the fields and hills along the shores. These were fine if you could get to shore easily. Most edges of the sea were rocky and too rugged to land on.

After three days journey along the coast of what is now Lebanon, the mountains appeared steep and close to the shore. Then unexpectedly, around a peninsula a wide swath of tall green cedars appeared against a brown mountain background. As the boat got closer they could see the blue-green water of a wide river flowing out of the forest splitting a wide alluvial plain. Driftwood covered the sands of beaches that engulfed both sides of the river's mouth.

"Here," Aaron said to the captain.

Both Sebek and Nakht agreed. Sebek recognized the river as a good port. There was a small cluster of buildings. He could get supplies here.

Nakht thought of the place as peaceful. The tall trees pointed upward like a field of gigantic green spears, dazzling and dense in their numbers. Behind the trees, black and brown ridges of mountain rocks rose like megaliths sharpened by a clear blue sky. The river split the trees apart and vanished as it rounded a bend higher up in the valley. Light from the sky came down between the trees like a knife cutting a green apple.

On the south side of the river sat little squares of buildings. Behind the buildings, afternoon shadows of trees ran in dark triangles into the forest.

The men rowed the ship straight in and up the river a hundred yards. They approached a long wooden dock. Seagulls flashed gray and white overhead crying in piercing screams. As they came along the dock's side, a ship's seaman tossed a rope to a townsman who, along with several others, had seen them coming. He quickly tied off the ship's rope to a barnacled post with a sailors knot. A town like this, surrounded by steep mountains on three sides and the sea on the fourth, had to be accessed by water. Further up the river Aaron could see a small fleet of wooden boats tied to another dock which indicated a fishing community.

The community had harbored large ships before, ships that carried away the big trees, lumber ships. The lumber from the cedars of Lebanon were a sought after commodity. When not fishing, the people cut and milled the trees. They split the big trees after cutting by pealing off the bark and allowing the hot sun to dry them rapidly until long splits occurred. Then they drove hard wooden wedges into the splits along the log until it cracked apart. The resulting planks sat stockpiled along the

63

banks waiting for a trading ship with grain and other goods to enter the river.

The sleek pharaoh's ship was not a lumber ship. It was different and created a stir of curiosity in the little town. The community of people grew in numbers and stared.

An older man came forward and said something in a language that Aaron could not understand. Nakht answered. The man grinned.

Nakht and the older man, the town's mayor, spoke together for a while. There were lots of gestures as well as the strange words.

Nakht turned to Captain Sebek and said, "This man is the community's head man, like a mayor. He says we are welcome to dock here and explore for minerals. He will supply us with a guide and transportation further into the valley. He requests baskets of grain in return."

"That is a fair trade," said Sebek. "Ask him if there are food and lodgings available. Tell him we have many fine goods to trade for lumber."

Ships, irregardless of size, traded throughout the Mediterranean. Restocking supplies demanded trading one type of goods for another. The pharaoh's ship bartered for goods with grain, and in this case, traded for a stash of lumber. When a port with plenty of grain, but few trees was found, Sebek would trade the acquired lumber for ores or whatever else he thought was a good bargain.

BOOK 3: Egypt to Crete

Negotiations were held in the community hall. Food and beer were served with Nakht translating. The bartering finished satisfactorily for both parties.

The ship's crew and the two explorers stayed in the village that night. Early the next morning with packs and their solid bronze rock hammers, Aaron and Nakht rode in a small boat up the river with a guide who pushed the boat forward with a long pole. The river narrowed and became swifter the further up they went. Soon falls and rapids ended the boat ride. The white frothing water cooled and cleansed the air. A hawk circled overhead screeching as if demanding to know who or what invaded its territory. The guide tied their boat to a small cedar that grew at the water's edge.

Aaron's eye caught a glitter of light reflecting out of a rock crevice a short way up the mountain. The flash seemed to be a good place to start. When asked, their guide, being a fisherman and knowing little about rocks and metals, could provide them with no information. He would stay with the boat while the prospectors climbed to investigate.

They dug their sandals into footholds and without too much difficulty climbed to the crevice. A thin vein of silver-gold crystals glimmered along the wall. The small crystals were multitudinous and almost square where they protruded from the rock wall. They vanished into a dark cavern. Aaron could see the vein splitting in the cave into several more fractures. Nakht thought the vein might be gold or silver. Aaron scratched it with

65

the pointed end of his hammer.

"Too tough for silver or gold," he said. "And the crystal angles are too sharp, almost right angles. But let's take a few samples. Maybe Alim will know when we return to Egypt."

They chipped away, collecting a couple of pounds, filling a small hide sack.

"We know where this is now," Aaron said. "If it's useful, we can send a ship and employ the locals to mine and collect more."

"The trees around here would be worth a trip back anyway," said Nakht. "Did you see the size and number? Did you notice all the building were wood? If these rocks have any value, along with the wood, the pharaoh's men will make a haul."

What they had discovered was iron pyrite, sometimes called "fool's gold."

The cavern, a fissure type, led them into a large space where the mountain had split boulders apart. Light rays from a wide break above lit the cave's floor. They walked further into a dimming hollow. The sounds of the river rapids ceased leaving them in dead silence. That's when they saw the human skeletons. Gray ribs, arm and leg bones scattered about. Three skulls looked blankly back at the travelers. They were old. Among the bones, crude clay bowls had been left. It could only be a primitive burial site.

"Let's get out of here!" exclaimed Nakht.

BOOK 3: Egypt to Crete

"Agreed," whispered Aaron. "This is no place to prospect."

Although people's beliefs about death and afterlife can differ greatly, coming unexpectedly upon human bones in a dark place excites a common fear. It physically demonstrates a proof of one's mortality, something we don't really want to hear about. The thought of death when seeing human bones is a common trait among *homo sapiens*. In ancient Egypt death meant rebirth–and dead bodies should never be disturbed. If you did not treat a deceased body with respect, its spirit, its ghost, could return and make your life miserable.

The unnerved boys beat a rapid path back to the river. They told the guide who said (Nakht translating), "I have heard there are spirits around here, but never really believed it. Now I do."

***

Although the downriver return trip was quick, the two prospectors did have something to show. The square cube-like crystals were a wonder. Sebek and his crew thought they might be magic. Especially because they were found close to a burial site. No one wanted to go back there, so all agreed it was time to leave. However, before leaving, Sebek was able to trade grain for twenty-four long, straight planks of the well-dried cedar which they tied, twelve on each side, to the gunwales of the ship. Aaron put the small sack of rock crystals in a corner of the shared cabin room.

***

A NOVEL HISTORY OF CLAY

After traveling north along the coast for several more days and finding no easily accessible landing sites, Nakht suggested they turn west and cross the sea to the island of Cyprus. In his earlier travels he had heard of rich copper mines in the area. If there was copper, perhaps there'd be other metal ores. There were no objections so Sebek turned the ship west.

After three days of sailing the ship approached Cyprus from the south and tied up at a stone pier at a place called Akrontiri Point. Just beyond the high tide line, a mix of of low buildings gripped the gravelly shore forming a small town. Behind the buildings, small gardens, orchards and vines traveled up the hillside which eventually turned into a mountain range. The early summer weather illuminated the mountains in pink. Green spots and blotches of vegetation peppered the hills and the lower mountain valleys. Higher up, Aaron and Nakht could see what they thought were mines. The mines weren't far away from the beach. Perhaps only a couple hours walk.

On the beach were people. Families with small children laughing and squealing in high pitched voices played in the salty water. Older men and women wearing wide-rimmed hats to protect them from the hot Mediterranean sun sat on reed mats drinking out of ceramic jugs with straws. Aaron thought the old folks were drinking beer, but it might have been wine. He had seen little vineyards here and there amongst the hills.

The bought brought the boat in close to the shore and tied up to a stone pier. Nakht, Sebek, Aaron and a sailor, who had once lived on Cyprus and could speak the language jumped ashore. They walked the few yards to the beach people. The sailor and Nakht did the translating. This time Sebek could also speak the language a little bit and joined in whenever he could.

As they got closer, Aaron noticed lively designs covering the shiny rust-red jugs. Many had lively figures incised in the sides. After forming, the pottery had been coated with a liquid mixture of iron and clay (a slip) and then polished with a smooth stone. The large amount of red iron oxide in the slip combined attractively with the incising on the ware to produce an assortment of designs. All the pottery was hand-built and typical of the Cyprus ware made at the time.

Later archeologists gave this style the name, "Red Polished Ware."

The beach people pointed to a large nearby building. Nakht, Aaron and Sebek headed toward the building while the sailor returned to the boat to inform them of what the plan was.

While the sailors stayed with the ship, Sebek, Aaron and Nakht went into the big building where the local market was held. Trades were made. Accommodations were arranged. Nakht asked around and arranged for a guide. The guide would take them to the copper mines.

***

The next morning a white-robed guide on a donkey arrived at the pier. He was leading two more of the sure-footed beasts on ropes. Each animal had a basket hung on each side. The two baskets would distribute the weigh more uniformly and thus make packing easier for the donkey. Aaron had often wished he had a donkey when he was gathering sand from the desert. The side baskets were a great innovation.

The three rode high up into the hills. Aaron looked all around. The morning sun illuminated a beautiful landscape: the mountains ahead, the little green valley behind, set against a vast ultra-marine sea that cut a clear blue sky in an endless line.

Almost immediately, along the donkey trail Aaron noticed cuts of shiny obsidian and also a bluish-gray rock called galena (lead). *This is wonderful,* he thought. He could collect samples of both for Alim on his return from the copper mines.

Further up, the hill became steeper and more rocky. The young prospectors now saw black smoke rising above the rocks.

As they approached the mine, a large cutout of greenish rock opened before them. Below men with picks and hammers worked with an irregular clicking and clunking. Other men, muscled and tanned, wearing only loin cloths, labored, carrying baskets filled with chunks of raw copper ore up out of the hollow. They dumped the ore in piles near two smelter kilns.

The kilns were brick and tightly built with small chimneys out of which the black smoke funneled. Black smoke means the fire is reducing, not getting enough oxygen. Hence, in order to burn, the fire must get additional oxygen from the ores being smelted.

As a result the green copper oxide (CuO) in the ore was losing its oxygen and becoming pure metallic copper (Cu).

At the base of the kiln a man worked a hide billows pumping air into the firebox. Every couple of minutes he'd stop squeezing the billows and add more charcoal into the hot inferno.

Although Aaron could not see inside, molten copper was dripping out of the ore onto a smooth ceramic collection tray. When another man un-bricked a wide hole at the base and with bronze tongs removed the tray, a gleaming red copper appeared. He set the tray aside to cool and inserted another tray into the hole.

After cooling he turned the tray over and with gentle taps of a hammer disengaged the copper ingot. He gingerly placed the still warm ingot onto a stack of cooled ingots.

The stacks of ingots of refined copper would then carried on donkeys down the mountain to the seaside village. There it was traded for the assorted goods from ships that plied the area.

The pharaoh's ship would take all the copper that was available. Tin, imported from Anatolia and other eastern areas, when available, would be fused with the copper to create the important alloy, bronze.

The size of the operation impressed the two. Smelting the ore on site revealed just how advanced the mine operators had become. And why not? Copper mining on Cyprus had been ongoing for almost 2000 years.

A NOVEL HISTORY OF CLAY

Nakht's suggestion to head for Cyprus had paid off big time. They could trade the lumber and baskets of grain for refined copper ingots. In this one place they could acquire enough copper, pure copper ingots, that weighted much less than the crude ore. Plus it took much less space on the ship. Back in Egypt the pure copper ingots could be melted and tin added to create the bronze so vital to the civilizations of the times.

Alim would certainly be pleased. They were delighted. If they could find a source of tin, an even more successful trip was assured.

On the return back the two prospectors stopped and collected sacks of obsidian and galena. Obsidian could be used to create jewelry and fine knife blades. The galena (lead), at least that's what Aaron thought it was (and he was correct), could be melted at quite low temperatures. Both young men thought Alim, being a master alchemist, would find the material quite interesting. (As history moved on, lead being malleable was used for water pipes. Later, it was found to radically lower the melting temperature of glazes providing easy melts and highly glossy surfaces. Of course, its detrimental effect on health was not yet known.)

"An incredible find," said Sebek as he watched his ship sink a few inches deeper from the weight of the ingots. "Had we gotten only the raw ore, the weight would have dropped the ship another ten inches. Nice call, Nakht."

BOOK 3: Egypt to Crete

The crew agreed. The lighter weight meant faster sailing. And the crew liked speed. The breeze of a fast moving ship cooled the sailors as it sped along.

Aaron stored the obsidian and galena in their room with the iron pyrite.

From the ship's hold the sailors removed a large number of ballast stones and tossed them overboard, since their weight had been replaced with the mass of copper ingots. They cheered as they pitched the ballast rocks overboard. The ship rose up as many inches as it had sunk.

"Beer for everybody," shouted Sebek as the ship left the Cyprus port with a hold of copper and fresh jugs of beer. "Where to now, my young adventures?"

Aaron and Nakht had already consulted. Nakht knew the waters. Aaron happily accepted Nakht's judgement. So far his friend had led them well.

"Let's go north," said Nakht. "There is a band of high mountains that are close to the sea. Perhaps Aaron will spot another interesting place. Then, if there are no objections, I would like to sail southwest to Crete where I come from. You will find it an amazing place. And they have imports from the western sea. We may find some very interesting substances there."

***

After another two days on the water the ship approached the

coast of Anatolia (Turkey). The Taurus Mountain Range rose quickly up with minimum of foothills. As they got closer, the mouth of a wide slow river appeared, dumping its fresh waters into the Mediterranean Sea.

The river's headwaters began far in the steep mountains. It traveled down creating a valley that widened and flattened out into a land that could be none other than the results of river deposits from eons ago. On either side of the peaceful river, clusters of wooden houses spread far up an idyllic valley. At the river's edges a mix of boats were tied to docks.

"This looks great," announced Aaron. "If we travel upriver we'll be really close to the mountains. The landscape looks promising."

The ship docked in front of a the largest building along the river. Community halls and market places were usually combined together in the smaller towns. Nakht hopped ashore, entered the building and spoke to a fat bearded man who was tending the counter. A variety of goods filled tables and counters in the big open room. After determining the local language, a dialect of Cypro-Minoan, Nakht asked the proprietor if any mining sites existed in the area. The man smiled slyly and said there was an old mine in the mountains that was still being used.

When Nakht's eyes lit up, the man added, "I have an ingot here. Would you like to see it? You can buy it if you want."

"Let's see it," said Nakht.

BOOK 3: Egypt to Crete

Aaron, who had followed Nakht in, stepped closer as the fat man produced a flat cake of shinny gray metal from under the counter.

"Tin!" exclaimed Aaron immediately. "Ask him if he has more."

As the store owner talked he shook his head and animatedly pointed to the mountains behind him. The conversation between Nakht and the man lasted for several minutes. Aaron gathered the man's name was Katach.

Aaron glanced around the room. Fruit flies crawled over some ripe figs and juicy peaches. The oder of bananas drifted from a dozen big bunches that hung from the rafters on twisted twines. A shelf of clay cooking pots, although lacking the finesse of Egypt's palace vessels, showed a simple style, the result of poor quality clays. In a corner were stacked amphoras of what must be beer. There were no bins of grains. Aaron surmised that the hot humid valley produced lots of fruit but little or no grains. The pharaoh's ship had a great source of trading stock in grain alone.

"Katach, here, says this is the only ingot he has. He said it came from an old mine higher up the mountain. It's called Yusuf's mine. The people who mine it are poor and are only able to produce small amounts that they trade with him. That's why he has only the one ingot. Other ships pass through and purchase what tin he has. He said the profits are good but infrequent. The mining community lives on a narrow plateau about five miles up the river. I asked him if it was accessible by a boat our size. He said yes, but the crew would have to row hard against the current as they near the plateau. It's right on the river's edge and has a dock. Further up the river, Katach says there are impassible rapids."

Nakht and Aaron reported back to Sebek. He agreed it'd be worth investigating. Sebek, who could speak some Cypro-Minoan went in to the community and arranged to trade grain for a supply of fruit, fresh meat and beer. The crew would be happy with the goat meat. Fresh meat had to be eaten within a couple of days or it would turn putrid.

Sebek also acquired the single tin ingot.

***

After stocking up, the ship headed up the wide river with ten oarsmen rowing easily. Little farms and gardens speckled the banks between thin jungles of green trees and vines. A couple of miles further up, the rowing became more difficult. By the time they reached the dock at the base of a plateau, the men were sweating from the exertion. They tied up to the dock. The few small crude boats next to the dock were dwarfed by the pharaoh's boat.

People gathered around. Never had they seen such a boat. They marveled at it's craftsmanship, the sleek lines and a size that seemed much too big for the river. The men on board waved and smiled at the people. Sailors had learned that more advantage could be gained by the language of friendliness than displays of superiority. This was especially true with countryfolk. Good people shared what they had. Confrontations, violent or otherwise, were to be avoided. After all, the crew was always outnumbered and not on their familiar water terrain. However, the crew did have weapons and knew how to fight; pirates did prowl the salty Mediterranean.

Aaron, Nakht, Sebek and two of the crew followed the locals up a short road to the cluster of houses that sat on the small plateau overlooking the river. The view of the cascading water in the mountains was breathtaking. White snow could be see on the mountain peaks. A gentle breeze drifted down from the tops of the mountain ranges, through river gorges and over deep-green treetops bringing a pleasant coolness with it.

Nakht thought, *these people may be poor, but the view is worth a fortune.*

Aaron thought, *these people may be poor, but they're living in paradise.*

Smells of open cooking fires in the little village mixed into and drifted with the fresh air. Scrawny chickens wandered about pecking at bugs and weeds. A few goats nibbled branches higher up where a trail began (hopefully leading to Yusuf's mine). The plateau supported a village of 200 people, young and old. It had existed for hundreds of years but only supporting a maximum of 250 people at a time. More than that would be too much for the tiny ecosystem to endure.

A teenaged girl helped a white-bearded old man across the village center to greet the foreign adventurers. He held his wrinkled hands up in a sign of welcome. His age and demeanor indicated he was the local chief. The wrinkles around his eyes led to his ears which had a few white hairs protruding erratically here and there. Above, waves of deep crevices flowed across his forehead. A shiny bald head reflected gold from the overhead sunlight. An occasional white hair stuck up and bent the light in little flickers as he moved. His deep eyes showed the wisdom of age, but no emotions.

The girl steadied the old man as they moved slowly toward the five strangers. The girl had long black wavy hair, unkempt, but still attractive in an alluring way. By her size and her body curves, Aaron thought she must be 15 to 19 years old. She, too, showed no observable emotions. The girl and old man seemed unreadable.

When a strange and large ship with a crew of virile looking men arrives unexpectedly, caution is expected. These men could be here to enslave the peoples. It had happen before and lingered in the old man's memories.

Thirty years ago men had come from the seas and up the river, landing at their village. They murdered the old man's father, the chief at the time. Using fear as a motivator, the invaders had forced the people to work the tin mines on the mountain above.

BOOK 3: Egypt to Crete

The men used whips and pushed the people hard, forcing them to dig deeper and deeper into the mountain. Small children were shoved into narrow tunnels and forced to chip out the stone incessantly. A ton of ore was taken at the expense of many villagers' lives. The community worked as slaves for their cruel masters for a decade. Eventually, the men left in their ship with a hold full of heavy ore. They had never returned, yet the people still lived in fear of their reappearance. Such is the lasting power of fear that people carry in their memories years into the future.

Unknown to the villagers, the bad men did not return due to a severe storm that drove their ship onto black rocks a hundred miles away in the Aegean Sea. Although the devastated community did not know, the greedy men had received their just due. All went down along with a ton of tin into the angry sea. That had been 20 years ago.

The evil men did leave something behind: offspring. They had raped women at will, leaving a legacy of shame. However, as life instinctively provides, the women loved their babies dearly and with such care and affection that the children grew to be kind and helpful adults. By the time the pharaoh's ship appeared one quarter of the village people had foreigners' blood in them, including the chief's granddaughter, Nina.

Sebek turned to the two sailors next to him and said, "Go back to ship and get two full baskets, one of millet the other of wheat. Bring them here right away."

79

"Aye," said a sailor. And the two left for the ship.

Nakht stepped forward and in Cypro-Minoan said, "Greetings. We come as friends–as traders. We have grain to trade. We are seeking the tin ore that you produce."

A undercurrent of talk spread throughout the crowd that had surrounded the group. It felt like vibrations both good and bad, an unreadable noise.

The old chief still showed no emotions. Then he said, "The mine is dead. There is little metal left."

When the two baskets of grains arrived, there was another murmur throughout the crowd. This time the adventurers could read the sounds. People were pleased. They were now smiling.

The chief's granddaughter whispered something into the old man's ear. *The grain looks good. The people hunger for grains. These men seem to offer, rather than take.*

"We offer this grain to obtain a guide to Yusuf's mine. My friend, Aaron, here, can magically find the ore if there is more anywhere in the mountain." Nakht put his hand on Aaron's shoulder and Aaron smiled at the old man although he had no idea what Nakht had said.

The chief's expression flashed a smile for a second and then said, "You will give us four baskets and we will guide you to the mine. If this magician, Aaron, can find more of the ore we can trade work for more grain. Is this good?"

BOOK 3: Egypt to Crete

Nakht translated to Aaron and Sebek. As he translated he skipped the magic part.

"That is fair," said Aaron.

Sebek agreed. He had guessed these people would like the grain. They knew it kept better than fruits and vegetables. Bread grain was a luxury for these people. With the grain, the winter season would pass with less starvation. However, Sebek didn't expect the old man to barter so well. He liked the old man. He seemed kind, but shrewd. Sebek thought shrewdly also. He could have bartered the chief down, but generosity would have a far greater value should Aaron find a good tin vein.

The ship's storage hold still held a vast amount of grain harvested from Egypt's fertile river soil. It grew so well that almost every year there were excesses. Thus, it was an ideal trading medium. Inexpensive to acquire. Easy to store. Not too heavy. A valuable trading good, especially to places like this where the climate and soil could grow little grain.

As spokesman Nakht said, "Agreed. Four baskets for a guide. Four days, a basket for each day. The guide must be familiar with the mountains. We will start in the morning. "

"A guide for four days. Be here at sunrise," concluded the old chief. He cautiously held his hand out. He wanted to trust these men, but past fears made him careful. He would take a chance. He hoped it was the right choice.

His granddaughter helped Chief Niko back to his tiny house.

Aaron surmised she was his caretaker. He watched them go. There was something about that girl, something resonated.

***

Early the following morning in the central yard of the little village Aaron and Nakht met the young girl along with an athletic looking man about the same age as the two friends. The air smelled clean and fresh from an ever so gentle mountain breeze. The sun's fire ball peeped over the mountain top. Shadows were long. A few people were up and about starting daily routines of milking the skinny goats and searching for eggs left by the wandering chickens.

"This is Zah, my older brother. He has agreed to be your guide."

Then she added, "My name is Nina." She smiled at Aaron, then Nakht.

"Zah," said Nakht, "can you take us to Yusuf's Mine so we can see what's going on there? Is it still being worked?"

"It is no longer being worked. A year ago my friends and I picked out a little ore and with advice from one of the old timers, we smelted out an ingot of tin. We traded it with Fat Katach. I can take you to the mine. It will take a few hours. What language does your friend speak?"

"Aaron speaks Egyptian. Why do you ask?"

"His shaved head and metal armlets. It is their style. For two years I sailed on a lumber ship with an Egyptian. I can speak it a little. He taught me words, or should I say phrases." Zah beamed at Aaron and spoke in a accented Egyptian, "Hello, Aaron. Welcome friend."

"What!" Aaron's head spun. "You speak Egyptian?"

Zah continued in Egyptian, "Yes, when I return home I teach some of the phrases to Nina. She learn faster than me. Smart girl."

Nina understood and blushed. A dimple showed on her cheek.

"I must return to Grandfather Niko," she said in broken Egyptian. "Time to wake him for his morning meal. Good bye. Good luck. We trust you, Magician."

She flashed a forced smile.

***

'We trust you, Magician.' That was an odd thing to say thought Aaron.

The prior evening, the chief, his grandson and granddaughter had discussed the proposition with other lead members of the tribe. The generous offer of grain had tipped their opinions of these strangers into a favorable light. Zah was the unanimous choice to guide the strangers. Not only did he know the area well, he could speak the strangers' language. The chief still cautioned Zah to watch the two prospectors closely.

Unlike Zah and Nina, who were too young to remember much

about the evil men, unpleasant memories of the past still lingered for the old man. He would send Nina to check on them in two days. Zah would leave a trail of three small rocks piled on top of one another. A fourth rock would be placed to the side of the pile in the direction they traveled. Zah said he didn't need to be checked on, but his grandfather and Nina would feel better to know that he and the others were ok. The mountains could be tricky. Sandals often slipped.

***

Yusuf's Mine had been worked off and on for over a thousand years. After the initial mining where most of the easy surface ore had been taken, the mine was abandoned. The indigenous people knew of the mine as having always been there and a myth of it's creation had been passed along for generations.

It was said that a muscular, bearded man-god, who called himself Yusuf, came from a faraway land between two rivers and with the help of many humans cut a narrow trail into the rocks. They took away many baskets of rock and left a hole in the side of the mountain. The tale of Yusuf's Mine had been passed on for countless generations. Storytellers added more details, making up fantastic stories of wonderful deeds done by the man-god.

Centuries later when Chief Niko was a boy the mine was rediscovered by the mercenary prospectors who determined the ore was tin. With the high demand of bronze by the civilized and

BOOK 3: Egypt to Crete

wealthy peoples of the Mediterranean, the prospectors decided to reopen the mine. Tin was necessary to alloy with copper to obtain bronze. Sources of tin were not too easy to find and quite valuable.

After the mercenary's boat left carrying the ton of ore down the river into the Mediterranean, the old Yusuf's mine closed as no one wanted to go near the painful place. After a several years, the necessity of trading goods drove a few of the younger men back to the mine. They extracted only small amounts of tin which they refined on the spot. The resulting tin ingots they sent down river to trade with fat Katach for basic goods. It kept the mountain community alive.

***

The three young men arrived at the mine at midday. They sat in the shade of an old stone foundation contemplating the beauty of the nearby waterfall. The falls split off from a larger creek and cascaded white over some ledges. They ate thin slices of flatbread and dates from the food pack Nina had prepared earlier that morning. After drinking from the waterfall, Zah spoke. "What do you want to see?" he asked.

"Let's get torches and explore the mine," said Aaron. "Is it deep?"

"I have never been in more than a hundred yards," said Zah nervously. "It branches a lot. It's scary–a person could get lost in there. There are stories of dead bones in there."

A NOVEL HISTORY OF CLAY

This was not what the young prospectors wanted to hear. Yet, it was just a story. Only a story. Where was the proof? Their previous experience with the bones and skulls was real. Yet, nothing bad happened. Perhaps bones were nothing to be afraid of. Animals have bones. People have bones.

They entered the mine with Zah carrying a torch of pitch pine. Black shadows of the three men moved with them along the irregular walls.

***

For two days the three men explored the mine. They carried a long twine and unraveled it as they got deeper. More than once their torch went out and the mine became pitch black. With echoing voices, one hand feeling the life line of twine, the other arm reaching out to the walls, they shuffled out following the twine.

The tin veins had been worked for over a thousand years. At the very ends of tunnels, when the torches stayed lit, there were only tiny veins threading into the rock.

It was noon when they exited on the second day.

Nakht said, "Not worth looking any further. The mine's been used up."

"Agreed," said Aaron.

Just then they heard shouting coming from down the trail. A girl's voice.

BOOK 3: Egypt to Crete

"Are you there?" it said.

"That's Nina," said Zah. "She's bringing us some more food."

She arrived carrying a large basket of supplies. They sat on stone ledges while they ate fruit and some newly made bread.

"I made it from the grain," said Nina. "The grain you brought is the best."

When they finished eating they decided to go swimming in the creek to cool and clean up. Zah said he knew of a good pool upstream.

The pool nested at the foot of a waterfall. The noise of falling water caused them to shout to be heard. The light mist given off from the falls invigorated the four youths.

"Looks great!" said Zah and he took off his loincloth and leapt in.

Nina also rapidly stripped and jumped in with a splash. Her head popped back up out of the water and she let out a scream.

"Cold as ice!" she shrieked laughing.

Nakht and Aaron looked at each other, eyes wide. This girl was wild!

They beamed with the abandon of youth, pulled off their loincloths and cannon-balled in with two splashes.

It was breath-taking. Snow melts from mountain peaks poured

the icy water into steep crevices, creating fast-moving creeks and falls which cut through the mountain rocks. Freezes and thaws split the rocks with Nature's everlasting power.

Above them, a huge hunk of mountain had been split off from last winter's turbulent rains. When Aaron looked up from the pool he could see the recent break. It looked interesting. He pulled himself onto the pool's edge. The surface warmed his feet and after another look at the mountain break, he decided to see what it looked like up close.

To the right, about 100 feet up from the pool, in the raw surface of the recent break, a wide line of dark gray-purple gleamed and disappeared into the mother rock at the bank. Aaron worked his way up the rocks to get closer.

Tin! Aaron's eyes followed the wide band. It split into still more veins. There was a massive amount visible. Where it penetrated the mother rock, there could be still more. It could run deep into the mountain. And until now, the tin had been hidden from men.

"Come look!" he yelled down to his friends in the pool.

"What do you see?" Nakht shouted above the waterfall noises.

"Tin. A lot of it!"

The three nudes climbed out of the pool and scrambled up the rocks to see what Aaron had discovered. Their youthful bodies reveled in the heat radiating from the rocks. Looking up, even Nina could recognize the discovery.

BOOK 3: Egypt to Crete

"Magician Aaron," Nina exclaimed, "you are powerful!"

Aaron looked at her and scratched his head. *Magician Aaron.* He thought she must be pronouncing something incorrectly. His eyes took in all of her body and he felt heat. He hoped it didn't show down below.

They all agreed a great amount could be mined right here. They wouldn't even have to dig a deep mine.

Zah understood right away that this could mean wealth and therefore, comfort for his little community. The grandson of a chief, Zah thought of his people first. Zah had the qualities of a good leader.

They climbed down to the pool and dressed as they talked about how to mine it and smelt it. Chipping out the ore would be easy with Aaron and Nakht's bronze hammers. The ore could be crushed in the nearby stone hollows that had been carved out by tumbling boulders and eons of time. The crushed ore could then be taken to the flat area of the old mine dredgings. Here they could build a kiln and fire and smelt the ore. This last part, smelting, was not familiar to Zah.

The earlier prospectors had built a small smelting kiln, but the smelting process took too much time so the murderous men had settled on forcing the villagers to carry the raw ore back onto the ship instead. When the bad men sailed off with the ore, the angry villagers tore the kiln apart in an attempt to eliminate the ill feelings the cruel prospectors had left behind.

89

The few old locals who could remember the old smelting kiln, although not with certainty, advised the young men who later tried the extraction process. The poor quality of the left-behind tin ore and a barely functioning kiln worked so badly that the young villagers abandoned the project after only obtaining a few ingots. Those were the ingots that had found their way to Fat Katach's store.

Never having been around to witness the smelting process Zah was intrigued when Nakht explained the procedure.

"Aaron and I can build a kiln, an extraction smelter. You can barely see what's left of one at the old mine site. We can build a better one.

"We'll divert the creek to make a flume to help wash and settle the ore chunks. Then we dry them and kiln fire them. We'll need materials and supplies to do it right," explained Aaron.

"I can help, too," Nina assured them. This was so new and exciting, she did not want to be left out.

"You always help," teased Zah remembering his little sister's persistent attitude as a small girl.

The enlivened group decided to return to the little community and propose their plan to the old chief. Without his approval there would be no project. Nina thought he'd agree, but Zah was concerned that the bad experience of the previous mining operation still hung in the chief's memory and might stop the plans.

BOOK 3: Egypt to Crete

Nina said with girlish guile, "I'm sure I can convince Grandfather Niko of the benefits."

***

After listening to Nina's granddaughterly persuasions and hearing Zah's first-hand experience with the two strangers, old Niko let his apprehensions go. He would allow his people to rework the mine if they wished. However, Niko insisted there be no whippings and the men be honorable.

***

When the two young prospectors returned to the ship with the news, Sebek estimated they'd be tied up for several weeks, perhaps months. He'd take the opportunity to pull the boat ashore onto the narrow patch of grass beside the dock. The crew would roll it up on logs and dry the bottom. In weak areas where the tar had split from the reeds, they'd patch it from one of the buckets of bitumen always available on board. Mediterranean sea captains were not fools. They sailed prepared for assorted disasters, a leaky boat was a frequent problem. Other emergency items were extra oars, extra sails, and, of course, extra beer. They did not have lifejackets.

While the boat was dry-docked, four crew members not working on boat repairs, were assigned to Nakht and Aaron to assist in the mining project. Communication between the locals and the sailors involved a lot of 'show and tell'. Words and phrases passed between the workers with Nakht and Zah often

91

translating. Before long communication was not a problem. There were smiles and gestures and an attitude of working in harmony as personal goals. In this way a regular crew of 16 mine workers evolved.

Old men and women who had been forced to work in the tragic mine enterprise now returned and, although too old for the hard work, gave advice based on their previous experiences. They had slaved to mine the ore which in its raw state (un-smelted) had been loaded aboard the foreigner's ship. They knew nothing about concentrating the tin by the smelting operation.

Nakht headed a charcoal-making crew. They gathered together a large pile of dry branches, placed them in a shallow pit with an air trough for a draught. They lit a fire, and when wood raged with flames, smothered it with dirt and sand. The fire continued to burn, but without oxygen the wood did not burn completely. When the fire died and cooled, hunks of black charcoal remained. *Charcoal burns much hotter than a bonfire. The temperatures reached are around 2010 F. Using a forced air billows it can reach 2300 F. Thus, it is an excellent fuel for smelting ores.*

Aaron looked around for a suitable clay deposit and found one along the washed-out banks of the creek. He tested it with the coil-around-finger method and found it was short. That is, lots of small cracks appeared in the coil. It was too sandy and would not make good pots. However, by adding sufficient chopped grass to it, the clay would work for building a smelting kiln.

92

He cut several one to two-inch diameter, straight bamboo reeds and bundled them together, winding twine around them to make a twelve inch diameter cylinder about three feet tall. He cut and tapped the bottom flat, then placed it upright on a level area.

He had some of his crew gather baskets of the clay while others went in search of grass to chop into pieces. The cutting tools were mostly obsidian. A few bronze tools had been temporally confiscated from the ship to use as well. The locals marveled at how well the bronze tools worked. Both Aaron and Nakht assured them that with a successful mining operation the local miners could trade tin for bronze tools.

They dug a pit and mixed the clay and grass, about 50/50, adding water as necessary to create a sticky working consistency.

Aaron, taking great gobs of the grass-clay mix in his hands, started at the base of the bamboo form and packed the clay about three inches thick all the way around. He continued packing on more clay higher and higher until the cylinder reached over 35 inches. The grass made the clay porous which reduced the amount of shrinkage. It also burned out in the kiln firing, creating an insulated wall, a wall that could take the shock and extreme temperatures of multiple firings.

When the kiln form began to dry and shrink (minimally because of the imbedded grass), he loosened the bamboo sticks and pulled them out. He had cleverly bound the sticks so that they would slide out easily. This left a 35 inch tall clay cylinder with a twelve inch inside diameter and walls almost three inches thick. It was firm, but still damp.

"I need a pointy knife," he said, and added, "Thin."

Gruf, one of the workers, handed him an obsidian blade, a thin blade with a saw-like look from the scalloped chips of its making.

"Perfect," said Aaron. "Now we make the fire-mouth."

He plunged the knife about 12 inches up from the base and with sawing motions cut through the leatherhard clay. First down one side, then down the other. When he had finished Aaron detached a horseshoe shape arc from the wall which he put aside. He scored and dampened the leatherhard cutout edges of the opening and with the wet grass-clay mixture built a protruding arched hood over the firebox mouth. The section that had been cut out and removed he would use later as a door which could be slid into the opening in order to retain heat and also use as a inflow damper to control the heat.

More and more of the miners stopped their work and gathered around. The magician was going to create magic. As he built the kiln, a primitive ore smelting furnace, the people watched. In his broken Cypro-Minoan, Aaron described what he was doing and why. They should learn; they should know. He and Nakht would have to leave eventually.

The leatherhard kiln sat out to dry for three days. By then it had dried completely.

On the fourth morning Aaron declared the kiln was ready for its hardening fire. One of the miners who was quick with a fire bow started the fire. He and Aaron fed the fire for several hours. All the grass burned out in white smoke leaving a network of tiny spaces in the clay which Aaron said was good because the kiln "needed to breathe."

***

The smelting firing took place the next morning. Almost all of the village hiked to the mine to see the magician make the tin ingots. Even the sailors from the ship had arrived. The atmosphere buzzed with anticipation.

To catch the ore when it melted, a sturdy collection bowl was placed at the bottom of the kiln with a tilt toward the front to guide the hot liquid tin into an ingot mold.

A half dozen dried bamboo reeds were inserted down the chimney. Then several inches of charcoal were poured in and around the reeds. Next a layer of the crushed tin ore, followed by more charcoal. Another layer of ore and then another charcoal. The alternating layers went all the way to the top of chimney. The tips of the reeds stuck up surrounded by black charcoal like feathers in a hat.

"What are the bamboo reeds for?" asked Zah.

"Air tubes. As the charcoal burns, gasses are vented out through the tubes. Heat moves up. The taller the chimney, the faster the draft and the greater heat. Of course, the bamboo eventually burns up, but while things are firing, there remains enough vent space to prevent the charcoal and ore from settling and smothering the fire." He added, "Fire must have air in order to burn. The more air the hotter the fire burns. When it gets very hot we'll fan the fire to give it more air and make it even hotter."

The fire began in mid-morning. As the fuel burned down, more layers of ore and charcoal were added through the chimney hole. The bamboo burned to white skeletons which crumbled and disappeared as still more layers of ore and fuel were added.

The melting point of tin is 450 degrees F, a very low temperature compared to gold at 1946 degrees and copper at 1981. Only lead at 621 degrees F came close. In three hours the first sign of melting occurred as the intense heat permeated the rocks. A thin trickle of tin ran down the collection plate and into the waiting ingot mold. It flowed slowly and glowed red.

The crowd oh'd and ah'd. A spontaneous clapping of hands filled the mining area. Nods and smiles were abundant. The magician Aaron had worked his wonders. His clay tube, the kiln, also glowed red from the process. To the people of this small village the kiln itself was a magic container. In it lived a genie, a genie of transformation.

The miners took turns feeding the fire, adjusting the door, raking away ashes and fanning the fire. As the ore melted, more was added into the top opening.

They worked the kiln for five more hours to get as much tin out of the depths of the ore particles as possible. In all, because the percentage of tin in the ore was so high, they produced a whole ingot of tin.

***

That evening, while the kiln and ore were cooling, the people returned to the village. Two of the least lean goats were killed and butchered. A celebratory feast arose. The night was young. The ship's crew brought several jugs of wine for the occasion.

An old man was heard to remark, "This is a far cry from the last miners. These Egyptians are great people."

Even old Niko had to agree. His decision (heavily influenced by Nina) proved correct. He let go of his reservations. Sebek brought him a big stein of wine in a excellently designed bronze work of art.

"This is for you to keep," he said in his foreign accent. The old chief beamed.

Aaron still wondered why they called him "the magician." He had only followed his instincts. The villagers smiled at him with enthusiasm and patted his shoulders as if some of his magic might wear off on them. Nina seemed exceptionally attentive. She stayed close by. With her limited Egyptian she translated the villagers words to him. She smiled and stroked his arm

97

somewhat possessively while translating.

***

Love does not have rules. Love is a feeling. In this little village, people did not marry. Once they trusted someone they shared their feelings openly. People who liked one another lived together. There was no commitment such as we have today. People were free to have multiple relationships. Sex was not the ultimate goal. Sex was something that just happened, something enjoyable.

"Aaron, Nina wants to be close to you, to be intimate," observed Nakht. "You should pleasure her while you can."

The more worldly Nakht saw the obvious. Aaron, still a naïve country boy, needed his friend's advice.

"What should I do?" he asked Nakht.

"Let her lead you. She is a free woman. She will show you what she wants."

Later that evening, when the party had turned to singing and dancing, and the villagers had loosened up from wine and a huge barrel of beer also brought up from the ship, Nina led Aaron to her small room in the chief's hut.

In the flickering light of a tiny oil lamp she put her arms around him and kissed him. He felt wonderful. To be loved so freely had never occurred in his life before. She pressed her body tightly against his and kissed him with her tongue. He could feel her hard breasts against his chest. He found himself responding by kissing her back. The warm wetness of their mouths awakened a passion he had never known before. She brought her pubis firmly into his groin. He answered her by pushing his now hardened penis against her. Nina led him to her bed and pulled him down on it eager to know this magician deeply. Aaron soon found himself naked on her bed, she on top of him rubbing and thrusting her body against his. This was Aaron's first time. He was completely smitten.

***

For three months the Egyptian ship rested at the dock. The boat had been patched and cleaned, cargo bays rearranged, and large casks of the clear and cold mountain water stored on board. With excess time some of the crew had "borrowed" some barley from the cargo hold and made a mush which they distilled replenishing their beer stock. The men relaxed. They intermingled with the locals. Some worked the mines with the locals.

A naked swim in the creek's pool at the end of a work day inspired the young sailors. The village women who labored along with the men also looked forward to a reward of a cleansing swim at the end of the day. Friendships were formed. Lovers came and went. Many were drawn into beds for which there was little resistance. It would be hard to sail away from this place.

A NOVEL HISTORY OF CLAY

By the end of three months the villagers had mastered the mining and smelting process. Twenty to thirty people regularly worked the mine. The vein of tin ore continued into the mother rock and a hollow appeared as the people followed its direction. At first an ingot a day was common. (An ancient ingot of tin weighed approximately 2.5 pounds.) Gradually, as the men and women had to dig deeper for the ore and travel further for tree branches to burn, the rate of production dropped to little more than an ingot every two days.

Sebek kept good records, distributing grain for tin. He would batter with the chief, but both parties knew it was a mutually satisfying arraignment. After the village had sufficient grains to comfortably last the year, Sebek traded with the precious Egyptian jewelry and fine pottery. Eventually the ship's hold had about 50 ingots of tin aboard. It was a good trade for both parties.

***

Sebek called Aaron and Nakht into his cabin. "We have enough ingots, both copper and tin. We should be heading on to Crete. Perhaps we'll find some new mystery rocks there for old Alim."

Nakht agreed. He was ready to travel home to Crete and see his family. He had been gone almost six years.

Aaron, who was infatuated with his first love wanted to stay. So easy it is when under the influence of blind infatuation to mistake sex for genuine love.

BOOK 3: Egypt to Crete

Yet love is much, much more. It is a force that includes the feelings of passion, affection, longing, joy, completeness, forgiveness, peace, friendship, kindness, caring, protection, faithfulness, harmony, bliss, and also the more shadow emotions of melancholy, blindness, heartache, dependence, jealousy, fear of separation, suffocation, insecurity, loss of identity, disillusionment, and rage. This huge arena of complexity illustrates why we have such a difficult time with a concise definition of love.

Aaron felt the force. It filled him day and night. He was wooed by love into an intoxicating dream that when manifested on the physical plane produced exploding fireworks in his body and rocked his soul. To see Nina, to spend time with her, blinded him from acknowledging he would have to leave. He had duties. He had a responsibility to old Alim.

***

A further comment on love: Love is both light and shade. It is yin and yang. It dances across the universe cementing us together in its awesome mysteries. Perhaps it is the recently discovered dark matter of the universe, a force that holds the rest of the world together.

As souls, we play with love to give meaning and insight into our relationships.

However, it is the shadow side of love that provides a necessary contrast that makes us recognize and appreciate the ecstasy of the joyous side.

Love is not sex. Sex is a byproduct of love, an animal drive so strong that it has, and continues, to confuse humans as to a clear definition of what love is.

***

"Aaron, there is a shadow side to love," said Nakht counseling his friend. "When animal desire blinds you, you have sex and eventually have babies. Children have vital needs. You lose your chance for adventure when you have a family. You stay in one place and do menial work to support your children. You become attached."

"I would love to have a family with Nina," replied Aaron.

"More than sailing the seas and exploring new lands–finding new treasures? Remember how it was in Thebes with old Alim? After a year or so, you got an itch to see more of the world and the chance appeared and you took it. Has not this trip given you a taste for travel, for exploration?"

"True," said Aaron. "I do like this journey. But I have such strong feelings for Nina."

"Feelings are fleeting things. Today you feel good, tomorrow you feel different. Feelings change rapidly. Do you remember at the pool when Nina played water tag with the other men? She grabbed them. They grabbed her. How did you feel? I could tell you were frustrated, jealous. That is the shadow side of love.

BOOK 3: Egypt to Crete

You cannot stop her from having fun just to be solely with you. She is accustomed to being with other young men. It is how they live here. Could you share her?"

"I do not think so. You are right, Nakht. I would be jealous. But I can't stop these feelings."

"Talk to her about it. Perhaps her feelings are not as deep as yours. Ask her if she would only be intimate with you. Would she turn aside her other young lovers. I may be young, but I've seen many cultures and attitudes towards love and sex. They vary from culture to culture. You've seen Nina's culture, their way of living, their openness to polygamy. Is that what you want? Even if you stay, your jealousy will destroy you."

"I think your reasoning is right, Nakht. I will talk to Nina."

Aaron acquiesced, but his feelings for Nina remained strong and powerful.

***

Nina rolled out of bed leaving a naked Aaron staring at her in the morning light. She had to check on Niko. She heard him stirring in the next room. Aaron wanted more intimacy, a time to be close, a time to talk seriously.

Nina's devotion to her grandfather bothered Aaron. He wanted her time for himself. He could hear her rattling pots in the kitchen area, preparing a meal for the old man. This is how it had always been since he first started sleeping with her. She was always busy–old Niko' breakfast, the morning gathering in the village square and the laughing and bantering with her friends, women and men. He was frustrated. Nakht was right. Aaron could not change the situation. He could not change Nina. He could not have her all to himself. He told himself in self-justification: *If you love someone, set them free.*

When Nina returned he tried to explain so as not to hurt her.

"The mine is fully operating and we have a hold full of tin ingots. Nakht and I will have to leave for Crete and then back to Egypt. However, the mine should produce a lot of ingots. The Pharaoh's ship will return in a year and trade for whatever you produce. I will really miss you, Nina. We will leave in a few days."

"I knew this time would come, Magician. We have had fun and I have grown to love and respect you as family. Your people have released my grandfather's burden of past pain and have given our village the potential to be a wealthy community. I thank you for that."

Aaron looked baffled. She knew. She had already accepted his parting.

"Since we have a couple of days left..." Nina smiled seductively and shoved the naked Aaron back on her bed. She slid gracefully in beside him. Her hand slid down and playfully squeezed his penis.

***

BOOK 3: Egypt to Crete

Sebek procured as much fruit and vegetables as would last for several days. He called it "luxury food." Nakht had arranged the details of the community mining business. They would work the mine and produce as many ingots of tin as possible. The community would use some to barter with for outside goods. The rest would be stock-piled in a safe place, hidden from outsiders, until the Pharaoh's ship returned in a year.

Aaron said a sad good-bye to Nina. She hugged him and a tear trickled down her cheek.

***

By the fourth day out at sea much of the remaining fresh food began to rot in the warm humid air. They tossed the bad foodstuffs overboard keeping the tougher-skinned citrus fruits and dates. The ship's remaining full stock of food, grain and ores sat snugly in the holds adding ballast to the flat bottomed boat. Had the ship a deep keel it would hold the course more easily. However, without the deep keel, the rudder man, and sometimes two rudder men, steered the boat southwest allowing for lateral drifting from the sea breezes.

After a stop at the island of Rhodes to replenish the food and water, the pharaoh's ship moved on in its southwesterly direction.

On the morning of the sixth day the wind picked up. It blew from east to west. The sailors hoisted the ship's sail to catch the favorable winds. With a strong wind behind they would reach the Minoan island of Crete in a few more days. All hands aboard relaxed and let the wind drive them on.

But the wind increased. Dark gray clouds appeared in the east. They swelled and billowed, soon dissolving into a wide wall of gray haze. A sprinkle of cooling rain spattered the sailors. The rain quickly intensified with the wind pushing it ahead in gusts. Water came at them almost horizontally. Thunder rumbled and lightening snapped and exploded all around the ship. Strong winds caught the sail, tilted the boat and pushed it mercifully southwest, the desired direction of Crete. It took two men to hold the rudder steady.

With the freak Mediterranean storm came waves–big waves. The boat was now a leaf in an ocean. The crew helplessly watched hanging onto the guard rails and whatever else was near.

When the boat rose to the top of a wave crest, Aaron looked down. Thirty feet below, the hollow of the wave trough was green and swirling with foam. Soon they were down in the trough. Aaron looked up. Thirty feet above, the crest of the next wave rolled white and quickly tore screaming down at them. The next thing they knew the ship was riding on the new crest and far below another trough waited to give the ship a sea-saw ride.

The up and down motion distorted Aaron's equilibrium. He hung on to the side rail and vomited. Had the storm not been so severe the sailors would have laughed at the novice. Instead they yelled, "Hang on tight, there's more coming!"

BOOK 3: Egypt to Crete

And there was more.

Usually the Mediterranean Sea is mild, big waves being only three and four feet high. A storm of this magnitude sent ships and sailors into prayer. The rudder men hung on for control. The exertion drained the men until Sebek ordered the sail down and the rudder handle to be lashed in one position. The power of the storm now drove the boat.

Between Rhodes and Crete are many rocky islands, some livable, many just rocks protruding out of the sea. Northeast of Crete are some particularly treacherous rocks. The wind drove the pharaoh's boat in the direction of the rocks.

Sebek ordered the rowers to take positions and heave away from the rocky area. The men pulled for their lives. The headway was little, but enough to avoid crashing into the jagged, black stone pillars.

The wind kept up its force pushing against the boat driving it forward in gusts of speed, slowing down between gusts and then speeding up with the next strong gust.

Suddenly a violent gust hit the boat sideways just as it was on the top of a white-water wave crest and the ship lurched far over to the side. There was a loud swishing noise and the cargo in the holds slid to the starboard. The displaced weight of the ore forced the right side of the ship to lean at a severe angle. People and objects slid to starboard. With all the weight on one side the pharaoh's ship could not upright itself.

A NOVEL HISTORY OF CLAY

The captain and crew along with Aaron and Nakht scrambled to the port side hoping their weigh would be enough to level the boat. There was little change. The pharaoh's boat was permanently listing to the side. Further, water was leaking into the ore hold. The asphalt coating had split. Rowing was impossible. Steering was impossible. The sailors began to pray, loudly beseeching the gods to save them.

***

And the gods came through. Three things saved the boat and crew.

First, the storm occurred during daylight hours. Although stormy, there was much more visibility than had the storm hit at night. The sailors' fears of blind helplessness in the stormy black night and the terror of unknown black-water graves was not present.

Second, the storm passed over in less than two hours. Although no longer subject to the severe winds, the leaning boat was left adrift in relativity calm waters. The sailors tried to move the ore back to stabilize the ship but when they entered the hold and stepped to the starboard to retrieve the slipped ingots, the ship tilted still more and men were left clinging to railings and the mast pole to keep from sliding overboard.

Third, and most important, by chance, two well-built Minoan Navy ships were returning from a mission of circling Crete as was their custom. A lookout spied the floundering Egyptian

BOOK 3: Egypt to Crete

boat.

The island of Crete is 16 miles wide and 120 miles long. It is centered in the middle of the Mediterranean. The Minoans were the first culture to maintain a navy. An island that depends on the sea comes to terms with the sea. The sea becomes part of their daily existence. The people learn its secrets. It is their life source. What they didn't obtain from their limited land had to come from the sea or elsewhere across the seas. Hence, the Minoans became superb sailors and discriminating traders throughout the Mediterranean.

To protect the island a navy was created. Because of the powerful navy, Minoan cities were unfortified. All the other kingdoms and city-states in the Mediterranean and Aegean Seas built walls to fortify themselves. Not the Minoans. It is a testament to the organization and power of the Minoan Navy that open and free cities were possible.

It is a minor miracle that the two navy ships spied the pharaoh's struggling boat. Had they not seen it, Aaron and Nakht's story would have ended here as a shipwreck on the Aegean rocks.

On investigating the sight of the floundering boat, the two Minoan ships determined the situation was dire and proceeded to the rescue.

When the rescue ships approached, an officer called to the Pharaoh's ship, "Do you speak Cretan?"

"Yes," Nakht yelled back in his native tongue.

109

A NOVEL HISTORY OF CLAY

"You speak Cretan very well. What is your status?"

"Inoperable," replied Nakht. "Not only has our cargo shifted, but we are leaking."

"We are coming alongside. Have your men transfer to our boats. Then we'll tow you to Zakros, the nearest port."

The Minoan boats, each with 50 rowers, pulled along side the damaged reed boat and cast heavy woven nettings across to the grateful Egyptian crew.

Finely crafted with wood, Minoan navy ships were sleek and built for speed relying on rowers rather than sails. Their boats were longer, yet more maneuverable than the pharaoh's finest. The bows curved upward in graceful arches with a deadly, pointed bronze ram beneath at water level that could easily rip open an enemy vessel upon impact. On an elevated and roofed platform in the stern, cadence callers, battle-experienced older seamen, used drums to control both speed and direction. A fast beat and the oarsmen rowed faster in unison with the beat. An alternative drum, with a deep base sound, signaled turns whereby one side of oarsmen would lift their oars while the other side pulled strongly, quickly turning the boat in the desired direction.

The navy ships traveled in pairs which made them especially formidable in combat. The navy patrolled the waters around Crete traveling from port city to port city. There were many sets of the big boats in the waters at all times. Pirates quickly learned to search for victims elsewhere.

***

The Egyptian sailors crawled over the woven nets to the Minoan boats, half the sailors to one boat, half to the other.

Once on board, the Egyptian sailors marveled at the masterful workmanship and order of the floating warships. Although a language barrier existed, an unspoken language among sailors of all nations soon surfaced. Things in common for sailors built bonds between many foreigners. Numerous unexpected friendships occurred on the open seas.

"I am captain Ahatt," a curly bearded man spoke up. He wore a broad rimmed hat and white linen trousers with a bright purple sash. "This is my First Mate Jon."

He pointed to a man who was busy organizing spaces for the rescues. Jon was dressed similarly to the captain, but wore a bright red sash. He had a thin boyish beard. His hair and beard were curly and orange.

"I am Nakht. I speak Cretan because I come from Crete." announced Nakht. "This is Captain Sebek of the Pharaoh's fleet." The two captains nodded a salute to each other.

At the name "Nakht," Jon's head spun around and his mouth dropped open.

"Nakht!" he cried. "Nakht from Knossos?"

111

Nakht looked at Jon and a big grin spread across his face. They bounded across the deck toward each other, arms wide apart and hugged.

"My little brother, Jon, I can't believe it's you. You joined the navy!"

"I did. We–your family–never thought we'd see you again. It's been at least seven years."

"I was on my way back to see you when our ship got clobbered by the storm."

Captain Ahatt recognized the long lost brothers' excitement and broke in, "Jon, you and Nakht can get to know each other again later. Right now I need your brother to translate. As soon as you finish organizing the crews, join us. We will have beer and talk."

"Yes sir, Captain Ahatt." Navel orders were commands. Jon grinned and excitedly went back to work, glancing over his shoulder at Nakht frequently as if to make sure he was not seeing a mirage.

***

The two ships towed the damaged ship for several hours. The navy rowers, accustomed to long steady stretches of rowing, pulled their oars with ease. The steady beats of the cadence drummer kept the oarsmen pulling in unison. Aaron and the crew felt at ease with the orderly process. The Minoan Navy, the world's first navy, excelled in seamanship.

BOOK 3: Egypt to Crete

From the bow Aaron watched across the waters until Crete, like all other islands, first appeared as a blue gray hump on the horizon. As the towing boats drew closer and approached the eastern shores of Zakros, the mountains turned from blue-gray to a dark purplish color.

In front of the mountains a deep green forest merged into a texture of jagged red cliffs. Aaron could see that a wide crack, a gorge, had split the mountain where a river had done its eroding work. The crack spread wider and wider opening into a large, low-lying valley. Rectangular patches of blue-green olive trees and grape vineyards speckled the low hills up to the edge of the forest.

Between the vineyards and the sea, a number of white structures appeared, one of which was the Zakros palace, a conglomeration of walls and rooms. Many buildings rose three stories high.

Between the palace and the sea's gravelly beaches a strip of shops and warehouses filled the space. A long stretch of docks butted up to the warehouses.

Nakht had said his home country was beautiful. Upon his first view Aaron enthusiastically agreed. He would be further impressed when he went ashore.

***

The Minoan Culture is considered to be the first European Civilization. Although the island of Crete is only 160 by 35 miles, it developed into a paradise. Being located in the central

113

region of the Mediterranean Sea, the Minoans traded profusely. Their main products were wine, olive oil, dates, a deep purple dye from a sea snail, high-end pottery and jewelry. They imported copper and tin, alloying the two elements together into fine brass products, both utilitarian and decorative. The quality of their craftsmanship excelled all other regions including Egypt. Thus, wealthy peoples throughout the Mediterranean lusted after the refined Minoan products, which in turn made for a wealthy Minoan civilization.

***

Pulling the damaged boat behind, the two ships rowed between two weathered volcanic cliffs that protruded out into the water. The steep cliffs effectively created a hundred yard wide entrance into a calm deep bay. Aaron could see young boys diving fearlessly from the high ledges. Other boys, waiting for their turn to dive, waved to the sailors in the passing boats below.

Aaron looked over the starboard rail down into the bay waters. The water was deep, but sparkling clear. From the moving boat he watched the bottom slide by. A bright green sea moss grew along low ledges where starfishes and sea anemones clung in dots of reds and purples. The orange humps of big seashells came and went. Green ribbons of kelp swayed to and fro in slow moving undercurrents. Schools of colorful fish glided through the waving kelp. It had the effect of a silent movie in an underwater garden. Under other circumstances Aaron would have dove right in.

BOOK 3: Egypt to Crete

As they got close to the shore, Aaron could make out people moving about in a vast complex of buildings–one, two, three and four stories high. The afternoon sun bounced white light off rooftops and walls in angles that seemed chaotic, yet stunningly radiant. The structure of the building-complex seemed to ramble haphazardly.

"How do you like Zakros Palace," said Nakht who was standing beside him.

"That's the palace? replied Aaron. "No walls?"

"Crete palaces are not fortified. No one gets by our navy. Crete palaces are actually building complexes, always under construction with the edges growing outward. As the population grows so do the palaces."

As if to prove Nakht's point, the echoing sounds of hammering and intermittent cries of workmen interrupted the slow rhythmic drum beating and the slapping of fifty oars pushing the navy ships toward the largest dock.

Looking over and beyond the palace on the lower slopes, west toward the island's center, Aaron saw a large green pasture with what appeared to be cattle grazing. Beyond that, a checkered pattern of cultivated olive trees, interspaced with darker patterns of grape vineyards, climbed up the gentle slopes.

Aside from a large beach area to the north, the bay's edges were lined with wooden docks and colorful boats. Nearby were big warehouses and a large market area. The sounds of busy people and the smells of spices drifted across the water and the hungry sailors salivated. They would get a good meal tonight.

As the boats neared the shore people waved and cheered. They loved their navy.

The navy ships pulled the damaged reed boat to the dock and released it. Sebek would have to evaluate the condition and determine what to do. The situation did not look good. *At least,* he thought, *we didn't loose any men or cargo.*

***

Captain Ahatt took Nakht and Captain Sebek into a tall building with brightly painted walls displaying porpoises, schools of fish, octopuses and sea-themed plants. On the top floor in a room with windows all around, he introduced Sebek and Nakht to Charn, the harbor-master. Nakht had come along to translate as needed.

"You are in quite a fix. What do you plan to do?" asked Charn.

The harbor-master, a rugged-looking man, dressed similar to Ahatt and his sailors, but wore a bright yellow sash that stylishly complemented his yellow beard. A gold chain necklace with a prominent circular pendant hung from his neck revealing a finely detailed sea scene. On low shelves beside Charn's big desk were miniature replicas of assorted sailing vessels. Most were wood, but there was also one reed boat similar to the Egyptian style.

Sebek admired the sleek Minoan navy vessels with their graceful

116

lines and efficient accommodations. These ships were designed to carry over 120 sailors with a cargo bay that could hold over 50 metric tons. Compared to the Minoan ships, Sebek's ship, one of the Pharaoh's finest, seemed crude and puny.

Sebek looked down at his broken ship from the top of the three story tower that housed the government official. His thoughts were a mix of thankfulness to be alive and how to repair his ship. The combination of a broken mast, several severe rips through the bitumen layer and water-soaked reeds looked formidable. The thick, hemp truss line that ran from prow to stern had snapped leaving both ends of the reed boat drooping into the water.

"I think it will take a long time to repair," he said. "We'll need to haul it out of water and replace the bottom with new reeds. Bundling and tying reeds takes a while. And we'll need a lot more bitumen than I have on board. The mast can be more easily replaced."

"Indeed the mast is the least problem," replied Charn. "However, except for a few plants imported for ornamentation, there are hardly any papyrus reeds on Crete. Likewise there are no known bitumen pits native to Crete. You would have to import those in order to repair your ship. It could take six months to a year or longer just to obtain the materials."

This is what Sebek feared. Not only was he was out a ship, but he felt responsible for his crew and the two young prospectors.

117

A NOVEL HISTORY OF CLAY

All would have to be housed and fed for however long it took to get back on the water. Sebek, although used to being in charge, foresaw the difficulties ahead. He began to look at his options. All seemed to involve a lengthy stay in Zakros.

Over the duration of the cruise Sebek had come to know Nakht as dependable, resourceful and intelligent. Nakht, Sebek thought, had the qualities of a leader, a ship's captain or a statesman. Nakht's ability as a linguist made him exceptionally well suited to international diplomacy. In fact, Captain Sebek considered Nakht better suited to run the ship than his first mate, Ugan. The mate knew his stuff, but lacked the finesse and diplomatic skills that Nakht possessed.

"We are in a fix, Nakht," he confessed to the young protege as they left the harbormaster's office. "We are stuck here for some time. I'm not sure what we should do. My first thought is to repair our boat, but there are no materials immediately available. How can we even order the materials with no way to get a message to Egypt. It's well over 200 sea miles away. What will the crew do while we wait?"

Nakht, unaccustomed to see the captain in a state of uncertainty, almost a state of depression, answered in an upbeat fashion.

"Sir, do you forget how wealthy we are? We did not totally lose our ship. And don't forget what's in the ship's hold–a great number of ingots of copper and tin, along with those other great trading items-gold, ivory, ebony, fine jewelry! All things in high demand in Crete."

Captain Sebek realized the truth in Nakht's simple statements. "My god," he replied. "We are rich! Why am I worried? We have more than enough goods to trade for whatever we want."

Nakht nodded, glad to see his captain and friend regain his composure.

"I have an idea," he said. "My brother, Jon, tells me that our father, who is a successful merchant in Knossos, has an extra ship almost completed. Dad was having it built thinking Jon would captain it, but Jon's love was for the more exciting life of a navy officer. So the unfinished ship has been in dry dock for a year. I'll bet Dad would sell it at a reasonable price. Jon says it'll be a good ship when it's finished. Wooden, you know–like all the ships around here. The gods of the cypress forests have given their best to the people of Crete."

"That is brilliant, Nakht. Do you really think he'd sell it?"

"Jon says that when Dad and Mom see me they will be so overwhelmed, they'll practically give me the ship. Of course, I could not accept such a gift. After all, I've been gone for seven years, a wayward son. I do have honor."

"How can we make this happen?" Sebek's enthusiasm lit up his sun-tanned face. Lines of delight spread from the corners of his eyes and a grin appeared that exposed white sparkly teeth that reflected like little stars from his mouth. He imagined the awe he would create in the Pharaoh's court when he return to Egypt in a marvelous wooden ship.

"We must go to Knossos," said Nakht.

"Agreed," said Sebek.

***

Arraignments were made. The navy captain, Ahatt, glad to be helpful, agreed to take Sebek and Nakht on the routine patrol trip around the northeast waters of Crete to the city of Knossos.

Captain Sebek rented a large waterfront building for Aaron and the crew to stay in while he and Nakht went to Knossos. The crew was to unload the broken ship and store the copper, tin and other items in the building. The gold would stay under Ugan's charge to be used for any necessary bartering necessary to support the crew's needs. The ivory, ebony and inlaid jewelry would travel with Sebek to trade in Knossos.

Senior Captain Ahatt and his "buddy" ship would be leaving with Sebek and Nakht for Knossos in three days.

***

Captain Ahatt gave Jon special time off. The auspicious meeting of the two brothers indicated the goddesses favored the two. How else could such a happening occur? After seven years! A rescued ship in the middle of the sea....

The following morning Jon, Aaron and Nakht set out to explore Zakros. The cool breeze and clean ocean smells invigorated the young men. Nakht wanted to be sure Aaron, who was now like a brother, could find his way around Zakros while he and Sebek were in Knossos. Nakht felt that between Aaron's simple Cypro-Minoan language skills, plus the fact that seaports were places where multiple languages were spoken, would suffice for communicating with the locals.

Already the Zakros seaport hummed with activity. The smells of fish and drying seaweed mixed with the aroma of cooking seafoods. The smells led to a small eatery on the dock that specialized in frying the catch of the day in olive oil and herbs.

The three ate breakfast by an open window watching the fishing boats and merchant ships rock gently against docks. Their rolling masts created thin shadows that danced in criss-cross rhythms. Two more navy boats lay anchored in the peaceful bay. Like the rescue boats, they looked sleek with dolphins and watery-themed designs painted along the sides and on cabin canopies. All along the long stretch of dock a cornucopia of hammer tapping, ropes creaking, saws buzzing and workmen shouting, mixed with the slurping noises of the lapping waves. Zakros was indeed an industrious seaport.

The white city-palace appeared to be under construction several hundred feet from the shore where the earth rose in a low broad plateau–high enough to avoid spring tides and storm surges, but low enough to be easily accessible.

Jon led Aaron and Nakht into the palace marketplace area

through a wide-open gate, defined by two immense, polished white columns that curved upward and outward. The columns were tapered and ended with smooth pointed tips representing bull horns.

Men, women and children were bustling about, many carrying baskets of fruits and vegetables on their heads. Display stands of foods and crafts lined the south palace wall in a rainbow of colors. Active trading was brisk. By the mix of activity, it became obvious to Aaron that the city-folk were appreciative of the farmers and visa-versa.

The hum of foreign voices bartering for food, goods and crafts filled Aaron's ears. He would have been overwhelmed if it were not for the many people who nodded at the young strangers and welcomed them with smiles.

Although the size and beauty of the city-palace filled Aaron with awe, it was the Cretan women that stunned him.

"Oh, my!" exclaimed Aaron.

"What is it, Aaron?" queried Nakht.

"They're beautiful! It's amazing here! The women wear their breasts exposed like,– like open flowers."

"I forgot to tell you, my friend," said Nakht. "It's the style here on Crete. Women are highly respected and honored. The patron goddess, *Britomartis,* came from the sea to guide and protect the harbors and navigation of all Minoans. Out of respect, and to honor Her, the women tie their bodices firmly under their breasts to point their nipples up in tribute. In fact, our culture is dominated by women. Although we have a king residing in Knossos, it's a matriarchal society. The women are in charge in most matters. Jon tells me the day of honoring *Britomartis* is coming after the fall harvest. With our ship in such bad shape, perhaps we'll still be here for the procession and celebrations."

"Women in control," mused Aaron, "That explains the softness, the beautiful curves everywhere–the paintings, the graceful metal work, even the pottery. So Beautiful. These people seem really happy. Their art shows it."

"Agreed, I've been away so long I forgot how special my home island is. Here's your chance to try speaking the Cypro-Minoean I've been teaching you. Don't worry about mispronouncing; this is a seaport. The people are used to foreign languages. Many speak more than one language. Some even speak a little Egyptian."

Aaron smiled. This place would be exciting.

The vast, almost completed city-palace extended back toward the hills. So large a conglomeration of structures, all linked together by roofs and halls, that Aaron and Nakht estimated the complex included over a thousand rooms and covered three acres. From two, three and even four-story floors with columned balconies, the affluent could look down onto a big courtyard almost fifty yards square.

A NOVEL HISTORY OF CLAY

Jon told Aaron, "The higher up the rooms are, the more wealthy you are."

It was a status-defining aspect of an otherwise integrated culture. Although there still were the usual classes of nobles, middle-class, peasants and slaves, the closeness to one another and the necessity of working together, produced a more harmonious community than most other cultures maintained during the Bronze Age.

The walls of the courtyard houses, brightly painted with flowers, monkeys, dolphins and other natural themes, butted right up to the courtyard enclosing it like a coliseum. Wide exterior stairs leading from the courtyard up to the higher stories periodically broke the solid-looking walls. People sat on the steps like theater seats during events in the courtyard. Also interrupting the smooth walls, many smaller doors opened out at ground level onto the yard.

At the courtyard's west end beneath a roofed section, a pair of large red double doors painted with a design of huge white bull horns dwarfed the smaller side doors. The doors opened to an arena. The arena, enclosed within the courtyard, was partitioned off by a thick wooden railing five feet high held up by sturdy balusters. The baluster posts were driven firmly into the ground and spaced a foot apart. A thin person could easily slip between them. A good-sized grandstand surrounded the ring where spectators could sit and watch during the annual bull leaping events.

BOOK 3: Egypt to Crete

Looking over the roofed section to the slopping hill behind the red doors, Aaron could see rolling green pastures. Cattle grazed. Stone walls enclosed multiple pastures right up to the edge of the palace courtyard. It seemed logical to Aaron that this part of the city-palace housed the stables.

The courtyard, like a central park, was the gathering place for processions, celebrations and sports. The poor and the rich lived together in the city-palace. Some workers left the city daily to work in the orchards and vineyards. Many worked in construction jobs and others as artisans devoting their skills to ornamentation of the white city-palace.

As in all cultures, a few people wanted more independence. They became the farmers and goat herdsmen who lived outside the city in the stoney hills. Others worked as loggers creating homes higher up the hills next to the cypress trees. Yet, all returned to the city-palace for entertainment and pleasure. The special celebrations of the patron goddess drew excited people with offerings from afar. The people believed a happy goddess meant prosperous times. And judging from the people and their refined culture, Aaron concluded the goddess was very happy.

Overall, there was such a hodgepodge of connected buildings, high and low, that the entire three-acre palace-complex melded together like a massive labyrinth of cubes, trapezoids and rectangles.

The Minoan people lived and worked intimately. They were well organized. Aaron could see from the many colorful wall paintings, bright clothing and fine jewelry, that fine art was much valued here. There was no surrounding wall for protection anywhere. The palace was not only a home for the royalty, but housed the majority of the commoners of Zakros as well.

Eventually, Aaron became accustomed to the bare-breasted women and turned his attention to the architecture. The Pharaoh's palace, although magnificently constructed, seemed square and cold compared to the Minoans. The Minoan architecture seemed softer and less rigid. It appeared to grow more organically. The interconnected rooms, like a maze, rambled around the courtyard and extended further out, still growing on the edges. Aaron noticed the tell-tale smoke of kilns on the north side of the city.

Aside from the women, the three and four-story mini-palace structures impressed Aaron the most. Multitudes of big ornate limestone columns, one directly on top of another held up carved and painted lintels, framing door openings and windows. Open halls disappeared into internal rooms from outdoor balconies. Thick colorfully painted beams running across the lintels held up ceilings, supporting floors above. The same system held up the roofs. Like Alim's laboratory, square open spaces through the ceilings allowed additional light and air to enter.

The easy breeze coming off the bay waters added a refreshing ambiance to the city-palace. It passed through open windows, doors and hallways, cooling the occupants from the hot

126

BOOK 3: Egypt to Crete

Mediterranean sun.

Had Aaron looked more closely he would have discovered a remarkable feat of ancient engineering–bathrooms with flushing water. By making double clay walls, water and drainage pipes were built into the walls between the rooms. The double-walls also reduced noise. Some suites, where royalty lived, displayed extravagant rooms and furnishings imported from all around the Mediterranean Basin.

For the next two days Aaron, Nakht and Jon explored the city-palace. They found wells and kitchens where food was distributed. There were nurseries where many older children assisted while other children helped do the many odd jobs such as feeding goats and chickens or carrying messages. There were language and art classes in the mornings and afternoons for children and adults alike.

Aaron quickly learned his way around. His language skills improved rapidly. The people of Zakros were friendly and helpful. His apprehensions of being left alone in a strange place with minimal language skills dissipated. When Nakht and Captain Sebek left for Knossos, Aaron felt reasonably comfortable in Zakros.

Nakht's brother, Jon, also left on the navy ship for Knossos.

***

It did not take long for Aaron to find the potter's section. Like the moth to fire, he had been drawn by the smoking kilns. The smoke came from several medium-sized kilns firing all at once. For each kiln a fire-master stoked in dry kindling, each man guiding his kiln temperatures upwards, competing with one another in a comradely game.

He had entered the potter's area by circling the outer skirts of the city-palace and following the streams of smoke. On the outside edge of the north side, Aaron discovered five burning kilns and two more empty ones forming a large semicircle. The fire-masters nodded to him as he approached the half circle.

When Aaron faced the kilns with his back to the city-palace, through thin layers of wood smoke he could make out a water well surrounded by lush green vegetation. A multitude of pots of assorted sizes and shapes protruded above the low grass that grew luxuriantly next to the well. Behind the well rose hills and a mountain of rocky crevasses and low shrubs. The mountain was once heavily forested, but now appeared denuded for it had been the main source of lumber and firewood for the palace and kilns.

The smoke and familiar roar of the kilns gave Aaron a nostalgic feeling. He remembered his home in El Kab. *How long ago and how primitive it was back then. Now, here I am in a foreign city—a whole new world. I feel good here, like I could belong here.*

Until now he had felt somewhat lost without his good friend to guide him. Old memories flashed before his eyes. Aaron drifted into a state of reverie.

Here was the clay, the substance behind all this. Here were the favored children of *Khnum*, the god who created people from the mud clay of the Nile, the potter-artists, the men and women who, like *Khnum*, turned the clay, the earth, into a myriad of things.

With thoughts of *Khnum*, Aaron daydreamed his history of past lives. He knew the earth. He knew the power of creating with the earth. His connection went so far back that he could sense the clay being formed by the grinding rocks of time.

"Stranger, may I help you?" said a voice.

Turning, Aaron ended his reverie and blurted out his best attempt at Cypro-Minoan.

"Clay here?"

"Come," said the voice.

Aaron followed the man from the kiln yard onto a covered porch. He was an older man, perhaps 60 or even 70. He had dried clay on his bare chest and up his arms to his elbows. The old man walked with authority. *Most likely a master potter,* thought Aaron.

The shaded porch held baskets of a wide variety of pots packed in straw. Aaron thought each basket might contain a different order. Many of the fired pieces had beautiful flowing patterns depicting octopuses and underwater floral patterns. Other baskets included cups and bowls, casually thrown, yet elegant with lively decorations on the sides.

Then he saw the huge pots standing in a corner. The big storage vessels (called *pithoi*) were at least five feet high. They were powerful in their size alone. Thick wavy straps of flattened coils passed around the vessels as if dividing the vessel into parts. Each of the wavy clay straps bulged out in four opposite places, leaving loops which lined up with the loops above and below. Together they formed multiple eye-holes designed for ropes to fit through in order to lift the full vessels.

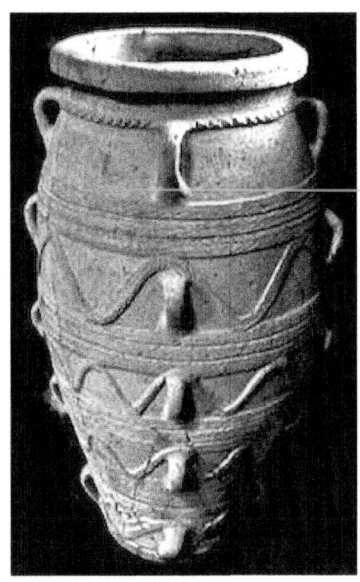

BOOK 3: Egypt to Crete

The big storage jugs held olive oil, honey, nuts, and grains when one could get them. To seal the containers a boiled honey-comb wax, which solidified as it cooled, preserved the contents.

Other pithoi with narrow necks held large quantities of wine which would be siphoned off into smaller containers (amphoras) to be used for domestic drinking or shipping as a trade good.

Aaron followed the old potter through a wide door leading into a secondary room where five potters worked five wheels. They were wheels unlike any he had ever seen. The potters, three men and two women, sat on the edges of three-foot cube frames. Each frame looked like a big wooden box skeleton. The potter's wheel-head was secured in the top center with a shaft underneath. Heavily oiled cords secured the shaft to four corners of the frame. (Aaron could see they were well-worn.) Attached to the bottom of the shaft was a large round flywheel made of thick wood. Beneath, the flywheel's center spun on a fired-hardened clay point.

The potters were kicking the flywheels with their feet which turned the shaft thus turning the wheel-head. There was no slave. No hand-turning stick. The wheel moved fast. The potters worked in a smooth rhythm. They kicked. Then paused, allowing the wheel to spin on its own momentum like a top. During this free spin, the potter formed the clay into shapes with his hands and special tools. Aaron thought of Seti back in Thebes. *He would love to know about this!*

A NOVEL HISTORY OF CLAY

In the ancient world, through observations and memories, travelers spread technical knowledge from person to person, country to country, culture to culture.

Looking about the room Aaron saw multiple racks of boards with rows of pots slowly drying, waiting to become leatherhard when they would be trimmed of the excess clay at the bottom to make stable feet.

Aaron pointed to the pots, smiled openly and said in Crypto-Minoan, "Good."

Several of the other potters looked up. One said, "Fun!" The others grinned and nodded.

The old potter handed a big glob of clay to Aaron, smiled and said, "Fun. Play."

What does he want me to do? thought Aaron.

He squeezed the clay and sniffed it. It smelled cool and musky. The old man watched as Aaron wrapped a small coil around his finger. Aaron balled it up and shoved his thumb into the clay almost all the way through. It felt good to have his hands in clay again. The pinch-pot appeared effortlessly.

The old potter disappeared through a door in the back of the throwing studio and returned with a woman. She was as tall as Aaron, slender and somewhat muscular. Blond curly hair hung down in ringlets over her ears. The rest of her hair was held up in a bun style with a bright blue ribbon. Bits of curly hair stuck out of the ribbon like spikes on a crown. Leather sandals snugly tied with cords could be seen below an ankle-length skirt of white linen. She wore no top. A clay medallion with an incised bull's head hung between her two round and tanned breasts.

Aaron tried not to stare, but her nipples stared back at him. They were dark brown and large like eyes. The aureoles surrounding the eyes were deep red like targets.

Aaron was caught off guard when the woman smiled at him. She then winked mischievously and further astounded him when she spoke in Egyptian. "I can see that you are new to our culture. I am Amelia. It is a *pleasure* (she emphasized the word pleasure) to meet you..." She paused expectantly.

She knew the stranger had been stimulated by her breasts. Why was it that the local men barely looked? But foreign men, well, they were a different story.

"Aaron. My name is Aaron from El Kab in Egypt," he spoke in Egyptian.

This is a very friendly place, thought Aaron. His self-consciousness dissolved with Amelia's smile and the wink.

"Ebu says you know clay. He watched how natural you are with it. He would like to know if you'd like to work in the pottery here."

"I'm not sure how long I'll be in Zakros," Aaron continued in Egyptian.

133

A NOVEL HISTORY OF CLAY

The woman turned and translated to Ebu who nodded and said something to the woman.

The woman turned back to Aaron and said, "Ebu says 'The will of the Goddess sent you here. She will decide your time.'"

The woman motioned to an empty potter's wheel. "That will be your wheel. Ebu says he will teach you how to use it–unless you already know."

Somehow it was already settled. He had been commanded in the name of the goddess by this old potter. Pleased (for he really wanted to get his hands in clay again) and somewhat honored, Aaron sheepishly replied, "I have tried on the stick-push-wheel and the wheel-with-a-slave-in-a-pit. I gave up after a day. I'm not very good. I'd rather hand-build sculptures. I have never seen this type of wheel."

After the woman translated so the other potters could hear, the whole studio broke out in laughter.

"What did I say?" asked a confused Aaron.

"No one here has ever heard a potter's wheel called a 'wheel-with-a-slave-in-a-pit.' That's a funny picture, an odd way to make pots."

Ebu spoke again and Aaron heard him say in broken Egyptian, "Old Egyptian style wheel. We fix it many years ago so it work without hole in the ground or slave. Crete wheel much better."

Seeing the many pots around him, Aaron had to agree. It was

134

better. The potter controlled the speed with his feet by himself. There was no need to coordinate with a slave.

Watching the ease with which the potters worked, Aaron wanted to try again–this time with a kick-wheel.

"Try it," continued the old man. "I show you."

The master potter commanded with enthusiasm. Ebu reminded Aaron of the old alchemist, Alim.

"First I demonstrate. Then you try on the wheel next to me."

Ebu hopped on the wheel's seat with the agility of a young man. He placed a grapefruit-sized ball of clay on the middle of the wheel-head.

Amelia translated.

"Kick near the shaft with both feet, right foot kicking forward, left foot on left side of shaft kicking backwards. Kick faster and faster."

Using a wet sea sponge, Ebu squeezed a dribble of water onto the spinning clay. He put his elbows tight to his sides and leaned over the clay.

"Only use your forearms. Always use both hands. Lock them together like this. Rigid like a vise. Think of them as a single tool."

Aaron could see the ripples of strength in the old potter's arms and shoulders. The ripples traveled down to his hands. Locking his two hands together, left over right, Ebu firmly started at the base of the hump of spinning clay. His fingertips dug into the clay until the clay was running smoothly with no bumps. Then he slowly brought a ring of irregular clay from the outside bottom to the top.

Amelia continued translating as Ebu spoke: "Use your fingers. Apply pressure at the base. Hold firmly until you feel the clay running smoothly against your fingertips. Then move the flat of your fingers–*not* the palms–pull a ring of clay up the mound until that area spins smoothly. Pause. You shouldn't feel any bumps or humps. Keep moving upward from the bottom and roll and press your fingers over the top until the clay becomes a single point. You should feel the clay run up between the grooves of your fingers. When the clay runs perfectly smoothly push down with the flat of your fingers to keep the clay in a low dome shape. Don't use your palm on top as you pull the lopsided clay up or the clay will bump into it and won't be able to move further up into the center."

Ebu forced the accumulated lopsided clay back down into the center of the hump. He repeated the motion two more times until the clay spun perfectly round in the center.

"Kick between each move," he emphasized.

When throwing on the wheel, centering is one of the most difficult and frustrating steps. Equally as difficult is kneading the clay so as to eliminate air bubbles and lumps. After

136

kneading, the clay should be well mixed, de-aired, and homogenous. If not well kneaded, the clay is difficult to center and throw.

Ebu went on to describe the throwing process. Aaron watched carefully with Amelia translating, but direct observation provided the most information:

> Centering, putting a hole in the hump, opening the clay, flattening the bottom, making the wall uniform, pulling up the clay walls, shaping by pushing out from the inside, collaring in the neck, leveling and fixing the rim, and finally cutting excess clay off the spinning bottom.

The demonstration inspired Aaron. The kick wheel lent a sense of using one's whole body to create a pot. He was hooked.

In a few weeks under Ebu's guidance Aaron learned to throw fine pots. He found himself in love with the soft clay.

The mysteries of glazing still intrigued him. There were so many things to discover. However, once he got his hands in malleable clay, throwing on the Crete wheels fulfilled him in such a physical way that it was the first thing he thought of when he awoke in the morning. It became his passion.

Aaron became a fixture at Ebu's shop. In order to spend more time at the pottery, he found a mat to sleep on in one of the shop's rooms. Four of the other potters slept there as well. Aaron's Cypro-Minoean improved, but he still felt left out when the others gossiped and joked.

It turned out that Amelia could also throw pots and frequently they worked beside each other talking back and forth in Egyptian. Amelia and her family had been brought to to Zakros from the west side of the island following a trail through the big gorge and settled in Zakros. Her father and mother worked on a cattle farm, a farm that raised bulls. She grew up on the farm. Amelia, who preferred clay to farming, kept a room further in the city-palace. She called it her sanctuary.

"Do you ever get lonely?" she asked one day as they threw vases on their wheels.

"Sometimes. I miss my family back in Egypt. I've been away almost two years. They have no idea where I am or what has happened to me. I look forward to going home and telling them of my adventures."

"What adventures are those? she asked.

The question opened up a deluge of talk. Aaron told her his story, omitting the painful part about Nina and his lost love in Anatolia.

"And I thought my life was adventurous," Amelia commented.

"Well, making pots is fun. There are a lot worse things one could do."

Amelia smiled. Then she fluttered her eyes and said, "Would you like to visit my sanctuary? I have some good wine you might like."

BOOK 3: Egypt to Crete

***

Aaron followed her through some doors and up a flight of stairs. Amelia stopped in front of a blue door. The white horns of a bull, not unlike the ones at the entrance to the city-palace and also on the red double doors, stood out, cleanly painted on her door. He noted the horn symbols. Along with dolphins and floral designs, bulls were common decorative features for the Minoan people.

He followed her into the room. The first thing Aaron noticed as he entered Amelia's room was a big window overlooking the courtyard. Light streamed in, illuminating a red and blue blanket that covered her elevated bed. She lived on the second floor. Aaron concluded, to live this well, she must have influence somewhere.

The second thing was a scent.

"What is that smell? It smells really nice." he asked.

"Oil of lavender and iris. I have used it on special occasions since I was a little kid. Both plants grew thick on the farm. Our cook refined the plants with a little olive oil and resin. You like it?"

"Yes," said Aaron and he took an exaggerated sniff.

"Then this must be a special occasion," smiled Amelia. "We can wash the clay off us over there."

Amelia actually had running water and a sink bowl in her

apartment. So marvelous was the technology that Aaron made a closer inspection.

"How does it work?" he asked.

Amelia described how the water arrived through pipes in the walls. She pointed to a large bowl sitting on a standing cabinet. The bowl had a hole in the bottom. She found a nearby wooden plug and plugged the hole. Then she pulled a plug out of a spigot that protruded out of the wall above the bowl. A stream of water dribbled into the bowl. Thus she had a fresh bowl of water whenever she liked.

When Aaron asked about the seat in the far corner of the room with the hole in the top, Amelia smiled and said, "I call that my 'sanctuary throne.' When you have to shit or pee you just sit there and go."

She chuckled at his uncomfortableness.

"When you're done, you wash yourself with fresh water and dump it down this drain." She pointed to a recessed lid on the floor beside the "sanctuary throne." She reached down and pulled a handle which lifted the lid exposing the open end of a three inch clay tube.

"When you pour in water, it rinses the wastes into the main sewer line and eventually out into the green field."

This is truly a marvelous place, he thought.

Minoan architecture had features far ahead of its times (by a couple of thousand years). Water from Plagin Mountain traveled via an aqueduct into the city-palace of Zakros, moving through clay tubes which ran between the double walls throughout the city-palace.

So ingenious were the Minoan engineers that not only was running water available for rooms, but a sewerage system also passed through the city-palace emptying out into a lush, low pasture area. By adding the gray ashes from the local kilns to the pasture sludge, the resulting mix of urine, feces and wood ash did not stink and created a very fertile soil.

The acid urine became neutralized by the alkaline wood ash. The main elements needed to make plants grow are nitrogen, phosphorous, and potassium, all of which were amply supplied by the sewerage/wood ash combination. With the addition of the waste water from the sinks and baths, the pasture region had become a jungle of flora, from grasses to wild flowers. Bees, birds and livestock thrived in the palace's wastewater pasture.

"Let's have some wine," said Amelia reaching into a cabinet.

From a shelf Amelia pulled out a jug. It had a fat belly with an octopus cleverly painted in black and white with a trace of orange all around the outside. The handle had a graceful curve, shaped and painted like an octopus tentacle that seemed to have grown out of the pot like a root on a tree. The pouring spout flowed out of the rim creating a wide "U" shape with a lip just thin and sharp enough to cut the pouring liquid without a drip

141

running down the outside after use. The form and octopus design flowed so well together that Aaron thought it was one of the most beautiful pieces of functional art that he had ever see. Amelia had made it herself in the pottery shop.

In a cabinet she found two goblets decorated with scrolling floral pattens and the now familiar bull horns. She filled them with red wine from the octopus jug. Amelia handed a goblet to Aaron. She held her goblet up to his and said, "To the moment. May it always be special and may it never pass...." and looking Aaron in his brown eyes took a sip of the wine.

Aaron tasted the wine, nodded and smiled. "This is good."

Amelia found some flatbreads in the cabinet and put them on a brightly painted tray. She motioned to the bed near the window.

"I don't often have guests, so I have no table. I just sit on the edge of my bed. I use the window ledge as a table."

She placed two trays of bread on the window ledge. Soon some small yellow and red birds landed on the ledge and began pecking at the bread farthest from the two humans. Amelia laughed and pointed at the little birds. "My friends," she said. "I feed them regularly. Aren't they cute?"

Her display of kindness tugged at Aaron's heart. She sat down on the bed near the window and patted her hand on the blanket beside her indicating for Aaron to sit. Aaron slid in next to her.

"Nice view," Aaron stammered as he looked down on the busy

courtyard below. He felt awkward, not certain what to do. He could feel her presence strongly. His hunger for a woman had not risen since Nina. Amelia caused a carnal lust to rise in his body. He wanted her but didn't know what to do or say."

She turned to him. He became very conscious of her breasts. She read his thoughts and pushed them closer until they pushed through the hairs on his bare chest. They felt warm–flesh against flesh. He felt himself quiver and he began to swell. Before he could register embarrassment, Amelia slid her arms around him and kissed him on the mouth. Her tongue wiggled into his mouth. She slid it back and forth against his tongue. Their slippery salivas mingled and they tumbled back onto the bed.

There was no going back. The two made love on the red and blue blanket, drank more wine, talked in Egyptian and made love again.

***

Although Amelia seemed to avoid talking about herself by turning the conversations to pottery and to his adventures, Aaron spent the first of many joyous nights in Amelia's sanctuary.

However, he sensed she was not telling him something. When pressed about her past, Amelia only said that she grew up on a bull farm and that, because her parents were required to work such long days, the farm had provided a nanny for the workers' children. The nanny was an Egyptian woman who had settled in Crete. She was the one who had taught the precocious Amelia to speak Egyptian. As part of her duties, the nanny taught the children how to make little objects out of the local clays. Amelia fell in love with the clay process and eventually found her way to Ebu's pottery.

It wasn't long before Aaron and Amelia's relationship evolved from lusty sex into a deeper friendship. When not in the pottery, the two packed lunches and explored the Zakros area, sometimes picnicking along mountain streams and other times at the seashore beaches. They hiked, they swam, they talked. The little trips reinforced their intimacy. The early days of infatuation and courtship, like all loving relationships, were euphoric for Aaron and Amelia.

Soon all Aaron's nights were spent with Amelia. He forgot about his mission for Alim and the Pharaoh. He smothered the thoughts of returning to Egypt. He even forgot about Nina. All was wonderful. The blindness of infatuation does that to people falling in love.

***

Meanwhile in Knossos, Nakht and Captain Sebek were negotiating with Nakht's father, Xantopos. He had a boat not yet complete that he would sell to Sebek as the Pharaoh's representative for 500 ingots of copper and 50 ingots of tin. That was about the entire supply of ore they had accumulated on their journey. Sebek, after admiring the uncompleted boat, countered with 400 coppers and 40 ingots.

BOOK 3: Egypt to Crete

"I must pay my workers," replied Xantopos. "I tell you what. For the 500 copper and 50 tin, I will have the boat completed and provide you with two sailors."

It began to sound like a poker game.

Nakht interjected, "How about finishing the ship and 450 copper and 40 tin. Then we take the new boat and one of your other boats back to Zakros. We row with two half crews. There you can pick up the ingots and load them onto your return boat. Then you can combine your two half crews and return to Knossos with the ingots–but leave us two of your sailors to help run and train our crew with the new boat. I don't think any of our sailors have had experience with large wooden ships."

Nakht's father, delighted to see what a barterer his oldest son had become, grinned and said, "You two drive a hard bargain. I will accept on two conditions."

"Go ahead. We're listening," Nakht consented.

"One. You take 100 amphoras of wine and 100 amphoras of olive oil with you in your hold. I'll provide the wine and oil. Your new ship is built to hold that many easily. Take the wine to Cyprus and trade for copper ore. Then take the olive oil to Anatolia and trade for tin ore. You say you have a supplier there–right? Present the ores to your Pharaoh and his alchemist and ask in exchange a full cargo bay of grain. Deliver it to me here in Knossos. I will recoup my expenses with the grain."

"I can see where Nakht gets his brains," Sebek grinned. "A

145

remarkably good plan. We get a fine boat, procure the pharaoh's vital copper and tin ingots, and you, in addition to the payment of ingots in Zakros, end up with a grand supply of grain to market. All with free shipping."

"You like the deal?"

"Yes," agreed Sebek. "What is the second condition?"

"That you take my youngest son, Kar with you. He already knows sailing ships, but the experience with you and his brother will be invaluable. He has the linguist's trait like Nakht. Plus, when he returns I will give him his own ship–providing you train him well. And Nakht, you may also find yourself back in the family business when you return."

"But Kar is just a boy," said Nakht. He remembered Kar as a scrawny 9-year-old.

"You easily forget, you've been gone seven years–long anxious years for your mother and me," he added. "Kar is now 16, older than you when you took that cabin-boy job. I was not pleased then, but now I must say, your mother and I are over-joyed to see you after all these years. I'm proud to see what you've made of yourself. So is your mother. You've become a fine man."

Captain Sebek thought so too, smiling and nodding his head up and down in agreement.

Nakht felt humbled. Leaving one's family and them never knowing what happened to you must have been quite difficult.

BOOK 3: Egypt to Crete

He had matured enough to know he would be anxious if he had a family and his child left without any way of ever reaching him or her.

"Agreed, again," said Sebek. "We'll take Kar on as a sailor and trader-in-training. If he's half as capable as Nakht, Kar will return with a cargo of grain. And don't be surprised if Nakht and I are with him."

The parties shook hands all around. A messenger was sent overland to Aaron and the crew in Zakros to let them know all was well, but it'd still be several months before they returned with the new ship.

***

The family reunion in Knossos called for a celebration. For the next five and a half months Nakht and Sebek had a vacation. They ate and drank and partied with many old and new friends. Whenever possible, Sebek seized the opportunity to accompany the captains of Xantopos's merchant ships. This way he learned how to master sailing in Minoan ships.

It took almost a full six months to finish the ship and snug the cargo bay racks with amphoras of wine and olive oil. The heavy weight of the big pointed jars acted like ballasts in the ship's hull.

***

Back in Zakros, the crew, out of boredom, had found odd jobs around the docks and on fishing boats. Aaron stayed and worked at the pottery. He was not at all bored.

During the next several months Aaron learned more Crypto-Minoan from Amelia. Although not perfect he understood most of what was said in the pottery. After all, the making of pottery transcends languages. It was communicated more by a show-and-tell method. Personal conversations with their nuances and figures of speech were a different matter for Aaron. Oftentimes, especially when Amelia was around, his co-workers would look at him, then at her, and back at him and grin. They knew he had a special relationship with the woman.

One morning Ebu entered the pottery and announced, "We need to make 30 large egg-shaped storage containers (*pithoi*) in the next three months in time for the *Britomartis* celebrations. They need to be need to be four feet high with shoulders and strong lips. We'll split the staff in half. Half will continue with the routine bowls, vases, cups, etc. The other half will construct the pithoi. Let's teach Aaron how to make a pithos."

The pithoi potters demonstrated to Aaron how to take the thick wooden head off the potter's kick-wheel and nest it on a low pointed ceramic chuck close to the floor. They showed him how the wheel pivoted on the chuck but tipped very little because slight tilts touched the floor.

To get clay (each pithos would take at least 200 pounds) the potters took a staircase down beneath the studio floor into a large underground cellar, the floor of which was covered with layers of dark linen. Big thick limestone columns spaced 8 feet apart held up solid wooden ceiling beams above. Across the beams the wooden floor of the studio wedged itself firmly in place. The studio floorboards, and thus the cellar ceiling, were moist from the daily washing-out of the studio. During the washing, water seeped into the floor cracks adding to the humidity in the cellar room below.

In the dim light Aaron could see a young boy pouring water over the linens to keep the clay underneath moist and workable. The area was cool and smelled musky from the mold that grew on the damp clay. The pithoi potters began gathering balls of clay about the size of basket balls. On long, thick cypress wood benches in the cellar they pounded and rolled the balls round and round until they became 3 and 4 foot long snake-like coils as thick as arms. After they had a stack of about 50 coils, each man draped two over his shoulders and carried them up the stairs to the waiting turntables. Storing and wetting the thick coils in the moist cellar was essential to keep them from drying too fast and thus not adhering to one another.

Ebu began to demonstrate how to build a big pot while he talked at the same time. The demonstration, being active, spoke better than words. However, here's a rough translation of the words he did say as he worked:

> Place an inch thick, flat clay disc about a foot or so in diameter on the wheel and center it by turning the wheel

marking the outside circle with a stick. This circle establishes the pithos bottom. Then start adding your coils fixing the first one firmly on top of the outer edge of the slab disc. Meld them together by dragging clay up and down over the coil joints. Don't get any air trapped between them.

Shortly, each pithos potter had applied the first two coils to his pot. Aaron's pithos was now about 5 inches high and thick like a huge dog dish.

Aaron and the others went back down and returned with two more of the big coils each. These coils were melded to the lower ones and Aaron's pot was now about 9 inches high.

Ebu stood next to Aaron explaining the process:

As you attach one coil on another, squeeze it into an tall oval so that rather than being 2 inches in thickness it becomes an oval 3 inches high and 1 inch thick. Meld it into the lower one like the first ring. Be sure to smooth the inside walls so the future wine or oil will pour out smoothly and not puddle in any crevices.

Aaron squeezed the coils into the elongated ovals and his pot grew two more inches without adding additional coils. He began to see how easy it was. He went down stairs and returned with another two damp coils. He attached, squeezed and melded. The piece was growing fast. It was looking good. It stood close to fourteen inches.

He was about to go downstairs for another set of coils when Ebu stopped him.

"Too soon for more coils," he said. "The bottom part must stiffen for several hours or the pithos will be too soft and collapse when the next rows are added.."

Ebu handed Aaron a long strip of linen. "Wrap this around the top few inches and keep it damp while the bottom dries. Then the next layers of coils will adhere well to the top."

It made sense to Aaron. Most potters knew that when fusing two parts of clay together, it works best to get two parts equally moist for the best joint.

While we wait, lets make some slips," said Ebu.

***

Ebu motioned for Aaron to follow him into a room next to the throwing studio. Aaron knew right away this was the alchemical room.

A large window let light onto rows of shelves holding lidded pots. A mixing table stood in the center of the room. Aaron recognized scales on the table. Several big, wide-mouthed pithoi sat upright at the base of the side walls. About half way up each pithos, and continuing to the top, a row of holes an inch apart had been made through the sides. Short sticks stuck out of each hole plugging the openings tightly. Aaron looked into one of the big jars. A layer of clear water could be seen about 4 inches deep. Beneath the water he could see clay.

"Reprocessing clay?" Aaron asked, trying out his Cypro-Minoan.

"Make ultra-fine painting slip. Watch."

The old potter stuck his finger into the water until it just touched the clay surface beneath. He pulled his hand out and held it next to the stick plugs on the outside.

"Water is down to here," he said.

He then pulled out the stick plug where he had indicated. The water spurted out of the hole much like a man peeing. Ebu had set a large bowl beneath to collect the stream of water.

Soon the surface water had been drained. The top clay layer was now exposed. Using a sharp-lipped cup, Ebu then carefully scooped off about 5 inches of the surface clay and dumped it into an empty, wide-mouth vase. The clay was pure, fine and fluid like a very thick soup.

"To make a fine slip (*in contemporary studio potteries the ultra-fine slip is called terra-sigillata),* first stir a cup of wood ash (soda ash) into a lot of water, heat it to help the ash dissolve, and then sprinkle in powdered clay. Stir it up really good. There should be an excess of water. It should look like milk."

Ebu lectured using his teaching persona. "Let it sit for several days. Don't stir the mix. Let it stand. The sand and heaver particles sink to the bottom first. Then the thick clay particles

152

settle next. Ultra-fine particles are left in a layer above. This layer is the desired layer. The water left on top we drain just as you saw me do. The layer of extremely fine clay is the base material of our painting slips. It's smooth and silky. Really flows nice and is easy to paint with. The clay remaining beneath the fine slip layer we send to the brick and column workshops. It's too grainy for our work, but ok for coarser brick production."

"What about colors?" asked Aaron.

"We add finely ground colorants to the ultra-fine slip and it's ready to use. Because it's a fine clay it shrinks a lot, so we brush multiple thin coats on leatherhard pieces. If you paint it too thickly on a bone-dry pot it will shrink more than the pot and flake off–so the pot *must* be leather hard. Ideally, the slip should shrink at the same rate as the clay pot. Several thin coats work best."

"What do you use for the colorants and where do you get them?" Aaron's geological curiosity had been aroused.

"We find and use the rocks with color around Crete. Other colorants come from other countries in trade. We tried using flowers and other plant parts, but the colors vanished when we fired the pots. We found that the rock colors stay, but plant and animal materials–we even tried blood–disappear during the firing heat.

"The rocks we use for white are tin *(cassiterite)* and limestone *(calcite)*. Copper *(malachite and azurite)* gives us greens and turquoises. And lots of iron-rich rocks (*hematite, magnetite and siderite)* and soils for rust reds, yellows and oranges. Blues, we get a from a lustrous blue stone *(lapis lazuli)* that is imported from the east (in what is now the region of Afghanistan). We're getting a deep, dark blue from a black substance we've just obtained called cobalt. We're still testing it, but it looks very promising. In fact we'll use some today. In short, Aaron, we try anything and everything. We test combinations and keep what works."

Aaron remembered Alim's processes of collecting various rocks and having his slaves spend hours pulverizing them into powders. He tried pulverizing once, but the work was so time-consuming and tedious that he left it for the slaves with an added appreciation of "slave work." Like Ebu, perhaps even more than Ebu, Alim tested day after day. One could sum up Alim's life as: *"What if?"*

"We had some cobalt in Egypt." said Aaron. "Alim, the alchemist, said it comes from way south in the lands called Nubia. He said it was worth its weight in gold. Do you have much?"

"No, but a little bit goes a long way," answered Ebu.

"How do you get black?" Aaron asked.

"Tricky," said Ebu. "Sometimes black (iron-rich) rocks work, but by grinding together the darker pigments we have on hand, along with soot, we come closer. Also, when the kiln's flame is

154

yellow we get a much darker black than when the flame is colorless or blue."

In obtaining a black slip (not a glaze), what actually happens is when the mix of metallic pigments (iron, copper, manganese, etc.) and black soot are combined with the terra-sigillata slip and applied to a clay surface, the soot combines with the silica from the terra-sigillata. A thin transparent silicate film covers the carbon soot layer. The silicate coating prevents the carbon in the soot from being burned (oxidized) and results in the black appearance–providing the pot is kept surrounded with burning fuel during the time the silicate film is flowing over and around the soot particles. The yellow flame Ebu mentions is an indicator that the process is happening. Yellow flame means the kiln is burning with insufficient oxygen. This is called reduction (without oxygen) firing. The fire inside the kiln will take oxygen right out of clays, slips or glazes–wherever it can get it–in order to burn.

Even today, potters overload a glaze with metallic pigments and fire them in reduction to obtain varieties of blacks.

"What color slips are we going to make?" asked Aaron.

"Red and some blue. For the red we'll use ground cinnabar. For blue we'll use some of the cobalt. The stuff is a black powder but is supposed to turn blue when fired. Shall we see?"

Aaron knew about cobalt from Alim. But he did not know that it had made its way to Crete. He remembered Alim saying that

155

cobalt could be found south in the country beyond the source of the Nile and that it would be worth more than its weight in gold.

"Quite expensive?" he inquired.

"Yes, indeed," said Ebu, "we had to trade an equal weight of murex dye for it. The dye's not something we use in ceramics. Too expensive. We had to get it from the textile shops."

Murex snails are spiny sea snails found along rocky shores of the Mediterranean. They are used to make Tyrian purple dye. Because it takes over 250,000 snails to produce a single once of dye and is labor intensive, it's extremely expensive. Only royalty could afford to wear the deep purple from the murex.

"Let's get started," said Ebu. "These fine red crystal rocks will make a bright red," continued Ebu. After pulverizing, we'll add in plenty to the slip to get a strong red."

"Are they cinnabar rocks?" inquired Aaron. "Where do they come from?"

Ebu liked Aaron's inquisitiveness.

"Yes, they're cinnabar. Although there are growths of the crystals near many of the hot springs, the majority come from across the sea northwest of here. Our trading ships acquire as much as possible. We Cretans love red. We obtain and store as much cinnabar as we can get. It's used in paint for wall murals as well as in our clay slips. The *Britomartis* celebration and bull leaping arena require a lot for red doors. Red is the color of excitement, of passion. The containers over there are filled to the brim," bragged Ebu pointing to three large pithoi vessels in a corner.

Aaron looked into one of the big vessels. It was filled with the shining red crystal rocks.

The chemical formula for cinnabar is HgS, or mercury sulfide. Mercury is a toxic substance. Cinnabar, although poisonous, is not as strong a poison as other forms of mercury such as liquid mercury which emits serious toxic vapors. Nevertheless, inhalation of cinnabar powder or constant exposure can lead to severe medical problems, even death.

In ancient times cinnabar provided vermillions and bright reds that other materials such as red iron oxide could not duplicate. Cinnabar was also mixed with oils and used as a cosmetic.

Another red came from saffron dyes. Although all right for cloths, it was useless for fired ceramic wares as it is organic and burns out during the firing process.

Ebu added a cup of powered cinnabar to a jar of the terra-sigillata and mixed it well. The smooth creamy liquid looked pomegranate red.

"Add a half cup of the cobalt to that jar," Ebu pointed to the second jar. Aaron added the black powder and stirred it with a wooden paddle. The terra-sigillata slip quickly became black. He wondered how this would turn blue.

157

They then painted a couple of leatherhard test pots with the two slips. In different areas of the pots they used single coats, double coats, and triple coats in order to see if the difference in thickness mattered to the final colors.

"Let's let these test pieces dry," said Ebu. "We'll have lunch and then get back to the pithoi. They'll have set up enough to add more coils."

***

When Aaron returned to his pithos, the clay had stiffened enough to allow him to add four more rings of thick coils. The big pot was now almost 24 inches high and 20 inches in diameter. Before he could add any more, Ebu interrupted him. Aaron thought Ebu was going to tell him to let to it stiffen as before.

"Time to paddle," the old potter said reaching for one of the flat boards hanging on the studio wall. "Turn the wheel."

As Aaron turned the wheel Ebu held a hide bag of sand about the size of a softball on the inside and smacked the outside of the partially built pithos firmly with a flat board. He moved the bag around and continued smacking the pithos walls. The walls of the pithos thinned to an inch and stretched outward in a smooth curved shape.

The technique of building with big rope-like coils and paddling while an assistant turned the low wheel resulted in large, uniformly walled pots. Of course, after every few rows of coils the pot had to be left to stiffen so as not to collapse. Whenever the working rim became too dry, wet linen rags were laid on the rims. Other times, to speed up the process, the rims were scratched and dampened with a wet sea sponge before the next coils were added.

Aaron worked on his pithos for two full days. The final form stood four and a half feet tall with a smooth curved belly that tapered into a wide neck, then flared out for the lip. Several thick clay straps had been fused at different sections creating loop holes for transporting ropes to pass through. The pithos would have to dry slowly for several weeks to be completely bone dry before moving it across the yard to the kiln for firing. Weather conditions affected the drying rate.

During his pithos construction work, Aaron became so busy in the clay studio that he saw Amelia less and less. After a while he noticed she had stopped coming to the studio. Had she lost her interest in him? She had always seemed warm and caring when they were together. He felt they had grown into a loving relationship. What had happened? He missed her. When he asked his fellow potters they merely smiled and said, "She has other duties."

Aaron began to re-live his loss of Nina. To ease the pain he immersed himself further in the clay. Needless to say, the *terra-sigillata* and new colorants intrigued him. Ebu noted the young man's interest with satisfaction. He hoped Aaron would stay at the studio but knew the youth planed to return to Egypt when the new ship arrived. Ebu wondered if Aaron's relationship with Amelia could alter his plans. It was obvious around the studio that the couple cared for each other. Amelia had told Ebu and the other potters not to tell Aaron about her "other life." She said she was working on a surprise for him.

***

The Minoan potters filled half of the studio space with the 30 consigned pithoi and an extra five as spares.

In the pottery business it is always a good rule to make a few extras for every project. Although prayers and offerings are made for successful firings, sometimes the fire gods are unkind to you. Backup pieces bring an additional peace to potters' minds.

Ebu said the big pithoi had to dry slowly in the shade or they'd develop cracks. On exceptionally hot days linens were draped over the pots and kept damp to slow down the drying process.

With the decreased studio space, the potters slowed regular productions and focused on firing the kilns. By the time the remaining stock of routine vases and cups had been fired, packed and delivered, the pithoi were ready to be loaded into the big kiln which could hold eight of the large pots at one firing. There would be five firings all total. Each firing would take three days. The woodsmen had been bringing in wood for weeks. A huge pile sat in the center of the kiln yard.

The amphoras would be finished in time for the *Britomartis* celebration.

***

In the studio the potters' conversations became more and more about the coming celebration. "You're coming with us to the goddess' festival," insisted Carii, a fellow potter.

Aaron nodded. He wouldn't want to miss this for anything. The other potter's had described bull leaping as the most exciting part of the celebration. It sounded incredibly dangerous. The bull jumpers must be crazy to tempt fate. Now he would see it live.

***

Throughout ancient civilizations uncontrollable forces such as storms, volcanic eruptions, earthquakes and floods were attributed to the supernatural–gods, spirits, ghosts, etc. Ancient Crete was no different.

Many cultures tried to appease the gods with offerings (even human sacrifices). Others attempted to negotiate with the gods through a priest or priestess (goods and services in exchange for safety, etc.). Still others were led to believe that the person in power (Pharaoh, King, etc.) was a direct descendent of the gods demanding obedience as well as offerings of tangible goods in exchange for protection.

Types of relationships with the unknown (gods, spirits, mysteries) include polytheism (many gods), monotheism (a single god), male gods, female gods, hermaphroditic gods, aliens (outer space), dead relatives, flora and fauna totem creatures. Further, the gods were constantly evolving with time and cultures. (It's still happening today.) The human psyche is marvelous when it comes to creating justifications and/or blame for things it does not understand.

In ancient Crete during Aaron's time, a hierarchical polytheism existed in a matriarchal society in which the main goddess worshiped was Britomartis. Over time the names and qualities of the gods changed to suit the circumstances of the cultures. Britomartis was associated with hunting small game on land with nets and as a protector of the nautical world of the Minoans. She later became synonymous in Greek mythology with Athena, the huntress.

To honor the primary goddess, Britomartis, all of Crete held a great celebration and feast once a year. It was the highlight of all religious rituals designed to maintain and protect the citizens of the island culture.

***

Preparations for the *Feast of Britomartis* filled the air with excitement. The people of Zakros gathered together and strung banners from the tall buildings. Food and music appeared in the eastern end of the enormous public courtyard. The bull ring was situated in the western end of the courtyard surrounded by a circular grandstand. An elevated, gilded stage, where the high-priestess and ladies of the court would sit and view the bull

162

leaping festivities, shone in the morning sun. A gold curtain hung in front of the throne seat.

The celebration of *Britomartis* was a time of jubilation. All people, including slaves, were free to relax, enjoy and celebrate. Young people especially loved this time for all non-vital work was suspended. Girls and boys, men and women, let themselves frolic in throughout the palace. Unions were made that at other times would have been forbidden. (There always seemed to be an extra abundance of births nine months after the *Feast of Britomartis.)*

On the morning of the celebration Ebu and the potters took Aaron to the bull arena in the courtyard. The sun had been up for several hours promising a fine day for the bull leaping. Aaron sat between Ebu and Carii a few rows back in the stands where they could see both the shrine and the red entrance gates, a large one for the bull and three other smaller gates for the leaper teams.

Bull leapers worked in teams. Along with the leaper and catcher, each team had five or more distractors much like the clowns one would find in a rodeo today. Many a leaper owed his life to his team's distractors.

When a leaper came flying off the back of a bull, the catcher's job was to "catch" the leaper, if necessary, preventing him from an injurious fall. Catchers were the strongest of the team members.

In the stands jugs of beer were passed along the rows. A growing chatter of anticipation filled the ring. Soon the bull leapers would perform.

***

A trumpet sounded.

The curtain in front of the high-priestess' shrine separated, revealing a female figure seated on an elevated, ornate gold throne. Her tall hat-like crown sparkled golden in the sun. A short-sleeved, jacket-like corset held up her exposed breasts. Woven like a fine harness, the corset gleamed of silver and gold which contrasted with her muted pink skin and further emphasized the priestess' nipples and areolae which were painted bright red. A long, flounced dress, also of gold and silver, hung from her hourglass waist to her feet. Aaron could not see what she had on her feet.

Between the high-priestess' breasts hung a large elongated, jeweled pendant on a gold chain. It had the look of a phallus. From her pale arms dangled a slew of gold bracelets that flashed when she moved her hands.

Aaron had never seen so much gold in a person's attire, even at the Pharaoh's palace. *Her entire costume must be really heavy*, he thought.

On either side of the high-priestess were the lesser priestesses. Next to them were the ladies of the court. They, too, were finely dressed with open corsets and flounced dresses but lacked as much gold in their costumes. Only the high-priestess wore the

164

tall hat-crown.

The high-priestess raised her arms with the bracelets sparkling. The crowd became quiet.

"Let the bull matches begin!" the high-priestess announced in a voice so loud that it surprised Aaron.

The spectators let up a cheer. The trumpet sounded again.

Aaron watched the big red door with the painted-white horns open. Out came a gray bull. The animal turned its head about, bewildered in the ring. It trotted about as if looking for an exit. The crowd applauded in admiration of the big beast.

"A small bull," declared Carii sounding like an authority.

It looked huge to Aaron.

"They'll get progressively larger as the leaping progresses," assured Carii.

Next, from a side door, the first leaping team entered the ring single file. There were eight, six men and two women. They dressed alike except for the leaper and catcher. Along with loincloths and headbands, they all wore soft leather sandals laced snugly up their calves. For additional support their wrists were also wrapped with leather similar to the sandals.

The leaper, leading the precession, a young Minoan from the north coast of Zakros, stood out by wearing a red sash snugly over his loincloth. He was followed by the catcher who wore a

165

blue sash. The rest, the distractors, wore white. They spread out, encircling the bull, forming a ring around the inside wall.

"Now the fun begins," said Carii.

The distractors ran in and out at the bull causing it to be annoyed. In frustration, or humiliation, it charged with it's head down at the leaper who patiently waited. At the last second he dove high up into the air over the bull's head and landed hands down on the charging bull's back. His forward motion carried him over the back and he landed feet first on the ground. He slapped the catcher's hands in success. The team exited the ring amid applause.

The second team entered. They were similarly dressed. The leaper performed the difficult move of grabbing the charging bull by the horns and flipping over, landing with both feet on the bull's broad back. From there the momentum carried him over and off the back where the catcher snatched him before he could tumble into the dust. It was an fine performance, but lacked drama.

Nevertheless, Aaron was impressed.

"It will get better," said Carii. "The first couple of leapers are just beginners. Wait 'til you see what's coming later."

The next jumper performed a move similar to the second. An impressive leap with a somersault exit off the bull's back. The spectators applauded and shouted approval.

166

BOOK 3: Egypt to Crete

The fourth bull entered the ring and trotted around the perimeter, obviously having done this before. He had longer pointed horns and was as massive as the previous bull. However, his quick trot seemed to have a more spirited step, a sense of *I'm in charge.*

The fourth jumper, a young man from Knossos named Xnos, and his team entered from a side door and paraded around the ring jubilantly waving and enjoying the applause. The bull stood in the center of the ring, turning his head to follow them around the ring and stared at the humans as if studying them with the thought: *This is my space. Which of these annoying characters should I murder?*

The distractors began to heckle the bull running in and out at it. The irritated bull began to move about starting and stopping, making short charges at the distractors. It became agitated, pawing it's foot in the dust.

The distractors spread apart leaving the leaper to face the bull. It leaned its head down, pawed the dirt and prepared a charge at the leaper who waved his arms about, taunting the bull in a signal of superiority. The crown roared its approval.

This, the bull could no longer tolerate. It lowered his horns and charged at the solitary leaper. The leaper took a few quick steps and jumped just a the angry bull reached him, his hands firmly grasping the two horns. Normally, when this happened a bull would throw its head up giving a thrust to the leaper who would do his acrobatic flip to the beast's back.

However, this time the bull stopped its charge short with the leaper in a handstand on its head hanging on to the horns. It thrust its head violently from left to right trying to rid itself of the man. The unexpected move caused the leaper to lose grip on one of the horns. The bull flipped it's head up and the leaper was tossed in the air.

The leaper's chest came down hard on one of the bull's horns and with a squirt of blood the tip of the horn came out his back.

The cheering of the crowd dropped to a silence. Then the crowd began to wail. This was not what was expected. Was *Britomartis* angry?

The team distractors managed to get the bull back through the red doors but their jumper lay mortally wounded in ring. The captain of the leaper's crew was left to do the dreaded job–put the dying man out of his pain. Howling "I'm sorry," he severed the leaper's spinal column at the back of the neck with a quick chop with a short double-headed gold axe. The stunned crowd became a mix of crying and wailing.

The priestess stood and raised her arms to quiet the noise. This was not the first time a leaper or a team member had been gored to death. She knew her lines:

"The gods have taken the admirable leaper. He was no coward. His journey to the afterlife should not be grieved but honored. Hail to Xnos! May he take his place among the great children of *Britomartis*. It is the will of *Britomartis* for life to go on."

168

BOOK 3: Egypt to Crete

"Hail to Xnos!" The crowd responded three times. The outcry gave voice to the turbulent feelings, releasing any sense of guilt that that was what many wanted to see–the dramatic edge of life and death.

The deadly accident sent a jolt of seriousness into the festivities. There was a short break while the dead man was carried through a side door on a red blanket stretcher. His team followed, walking with their heads down. The empty bull ring seemed hollow and depressing. The wailing of the leaper's family rose above the quiet onlookers.

From her seat on the gilded shrine the high priestess rose. She lifted her arms and, gaining control of the situation, said, "Let us go on to the next and final jumper. Let *Britomartis* be honored."

"I can't believe they will go on," said the stunned Aaron.

"It has happened many times. I don't think anyone gets used to it," said Carii. "It's what makes bull leaping so exciting. You never know...."

Before long the trumpet sounded again. The gate keepers pulled open the red doors. The bull that trotted into the arena was gigantic, white with dappled brown spots. Aaron did not know bulls could get so big.

"Now there's a bull!" exclaimed Carii.

The huge animal held his head high and paraded around the ring with authority. It's long horns were wide and painted with red

169

and black vertical stripes. The horns rose high and veered forward with a little dip before they ended in deadly points. Its neck and shoulders fused together, thick with muscles that rippled into a back broad enough to fit two full sized kickwheels.

The crowd's mood swung back into excitement as the great beast trotted about the ring. The loss of the previous leaper, although not forgotten, had been appeased through the tribute of the high-priestess and the people's three whole-hearted 'hails'.

The sight of the giant bull strutting about the ring refocused the spectators. In the eyes of the Minoans the bull represented the sun and the power of light, a masculine symbol of might. Bull leaping exemplified the power of man over nature.

"Wow," said Aaron. "That's a monster. Who'd want to jump over a bull like that?"

A side door opened and the final team filed into the arena. First the catcher in blue. Then eight distractors. And finally, wearing a scarlet red loin cloth and a scarlet headband came the final jumper, a woman.

She was tall and muscular and held her head high. The afternoon sun lit up bright yellow ringlets that leaked out of her headband and down her neck like a yellow collar.

Aaron's heart stopped. He knew that body so well. He remembered the curves, the long legs, firm breasts and the wonderful halo of golden hair.

"Amelia!" he gasped. And he feared for Amelia's life. The last leaper had died horribly and the picture had not left his mind.

"No!" he cried in shock and dread.

Ebu, who had been sitting calmly on Aaron's right, reached over and patted Aaron's knee. "Have faith my Egyptian friend. Amelia is not new at this." His touch was reassuring. Aaron was dumbfounded.

Amelia waved to the cheering crowd. The bull snorted and pawed the ground watching the woman wearing the scarlet sash with curiosity. *Who is this?* He had known women before when he was raised on the farm. They had been friendly and brought him food. *Where was the food?*

The distractors began their tantalizing dance. They ran in and out teasing the beast with quick shouts. The annoyed bull swung its head about watching the puny distractors with an air of: *Is that the best you can do?*

It turned its big head back to the leaper, the woman with the red sash. Something about her confused him. Ignoring the distractors the bull pawed the dirt facing the leaper.

Amelia swung her arms in a wide circle. The confused bull pawed the dirt again. Amelia waved her arms in the circle motion again as if a signal.

The bull was ready. He took a step toward Amelia, began a trot, picked up speed and then charged. The distance might have been

171

fifty feet. The bull quickly closed the space with its head down.

This was the moment all bull leapers both exalted and feared, the moment where the edges of life and death meet. Timing was everything. Too soon and one could miss the grip and be trampled to death. Too late and the horns would catch you in the air and stab you.

Amelia showed patience. When the bull was ten feet away she took two quick steps and gracefully dove onto the bull's head grasping high up on the horns with both hands. She dropped her elbows around the outer sides of the horns in a secure grip.

The bull responded by quickly jerking it's massive head up high. Amelia road the motion upward. At the apex her feet shot up and she released her grip flying high into the air. She spun one and a half times and landed with both feet planted on the broad back. Her motion continued with double somersault which ended on her feet just in front of the catcher.

The performance of a one and a half somersault followed by a double had never been seen before.

The crowd was on its feet and let out an explosion of sound that could be heard by the sailors who had stayed on ships at the docks. Whatever happened must be incredible to generate such a roar. The sound of such great excitement caused many sailors on the boats to turn their heads toward the palace, regretting their decisions not to attend the bull leaping performance.

However, there were two men who had made it from Knossos in

a new ship in time to attend, Nakht and Captain Sebek. Although they did not know Amelia, they were astounded.

The continuous roar of the grandstand spectators deafened the cries of the team distractors who desperately tried to warn Amelia that the bull had turned around and was heading toward Amelia's back.

The bull had lowered its horns and was preparing a second charge at Amelia. It began its charge.

At last, from the frantic motions of her team members, she realized what was happening and turned to face the charging bull. Could she leap again? It was coming fast. Could she jump in time?

Aaron, along with the crowd, screamed in horror.

"No! No!" he cried. "Get out of the way!"

However, Amelia stood her ground and held up both hands, palms out, as if to stop the charging beast.

Miraculously, the bull stopped, braking with its front hoofs stirring up a spray of dirt. He was inches away. Amelia reached over and touched his nose. The bull stood motionless.

This was an unheard of move. How could she stop a charging bull, a monster of an animal with just her hands?

The stunned spectators went silent. Amelia led the subdued bull to the red gate and it entered quietly. Then the crowd went crazy with cheering. They had just witnessed something miraculous. Surely, Amelia had the divine protection and power of a goddess, of *Britomartis* herself.

In the middle of the ring, amidst the continuous cheering, Amelia took off her red headband and slid it over her arm like a bracelet. Amelia shook her head vigorously, fluffing up her curls until they surrounded her head and face. She radiated like the sun.

Amelia strode across the arena in the direction of Ebu and the potters parting her unrestrained hair using her fingers as a comb. Yellow ringlets hung in front of her ears and over her shoulders. The crowd became silent. *What was she doing?*

Aaron felt relief, a yearning and a loss all at once. His memories of Amelia's little room and the happy times they had spent together tore at him. Why she had chosen him as a lover and friend, he did not know. She had made him happy. Perhaps it was a whim on her part. She had used him and was finished with him. Amelia was a mystery. She was far out of his class.

From the bull ring Amelia scanned the spectators until she saw Aaron in the crowd of spectators. She smiled brightly. She slid the headband off her arm and with a quick flick of her hand, tossed it straight over the grandstand fence striking Aaron in the chest. Aaron automatically grabbed it–either to protect himself– or to catch a wanted gift.

The crowd shouted its approval.

174

BOOK 3: Egypt to Crete

Carii and the other potters nudged Aaron. "You have been chosen!"

Stunned, Aaron said, "For what?"

"To be Amelia's escort during the rest of the celebrations."

Carii pulled a reluctant Aaron to the baluster fence and pushed him between the posts into the bull arena where Amelia stood.

He felt all eyes on him. His knees felt weak as he walked over to Amelia.

"What's going to happen next?" he said in Egyptian.

She put her arms around him and kissed him much to the delight of the crowd. Before he could register embarrassment, two of Amelia's bull dancer partners arrived with containers of red cinnabar paint.

"Relax Aaron, they are going to paint you. Don't worry. I will clean it off you later tonight." She winked a promising look. "Thoroughly," she added.

With such a promise, the stunned Aaron allowed himself to be painted red. Then another bull dancer arrived with a white paint and painted two bull horns over the red on his bare chest.

When the dancers stepped back, the crowd roared their approval. Amelia took his hand in hers and raised it up in homage to the mother-goddess *Britomartis*.

In turn, the high priestess, acting on behalf of *Britomartis*, rose from her seat and raised both her arms. Her bracelets sparkled. The crowd became silent. She spoke:

"The Goddess recognizes Amelia as the greatest of bull leapers. Many years ago she was brought to Crete with her parents from Athens as slaves. While her parents worked on the Bull Farm, Amelia grew into a woman, a woman without fear, a woman with skills above average. Only the Goddess could have marked a slave's destiny as a bull leaper. We have seen her perform in the past and rewarded her as seen fit for a valued slave. Today, the Goddess releases Amelia and her family from slave status and welcomes the great bull leaper to take the test for priestess-hood."

The crowd responded with cheers.

The high priestess waved for the couple to climb the stairs to her platform. They were to sit beside her. Attendants brought them each goblets of wine and platters of food. The goblets were well-balanced, thin, with red and blue floral designs playfully racing around the cup part. Along with steamed lobster tails and broiled rockfish, honeyed breads and seaweed-roasted goat were served on familiar ceramic plates. The same red and blue floral patterns danced around the plate rims. Aaron recognized the designs from the pottery studio.

Quickly, the celebration spilled into familiar the court yard with food and drink accompanied with music and dancing. When the party reached a frenzy, the High Priestess stood and raised her arms for silence. The crowd quieted and waited expectantly. All eyes were on her.

"By the will of the mother-goddess, *Britomartis*, who has chosen the bull leaper, Amelia Zakroos, for the highest honor," she commanded speaking loudly so as to reach the far ends of the courtyard and the highest overlooking balconies of people. "The priestess-hood welcomes Amelia to be tested. Do you accept the challenge?"

Amelia stood and answered the only way possible. "Yes," she said. To become a priestess in ancient Crete, when offered, meant both abundance and sacrifice. She had been chosen by the goddess. Her performance in the bull court proved it.

Two woven baskets were carried in by two more priestesses. They placed the baskets on either side of Amelia.

"Does the goddess *Britomartis* accept Amelia Zakroos as Her sister?"

Amelia bent down and put a hand in each basket. She could feel the dry scales and slithering movements of the creatures within. Gently she slid her hands out of the basket with a wiggling snake in each one. She held them up high for all to see. The snakes had not bitten her. She had been accepted.

The golden high-priestess spoke in her loud voice, "Henceforth, Amelia shall perform the duties of a priestess of *Britomartis*. Congratulations to the greatest bull leaper we have ever seen."

The crowd became exuberant, standing and applauding.

Amelia carefully placed the snakes back into their baskets. She took Aaron's hand and walked with him down the steeps into a group of well-wishers. Both Aaron and Amelia were hugged and kissed repeatedly.

"Do not be embarrassed, Aaron," Amelia whispered into his ear. "Even though the tides of fate bring us together and push us apart, I will always love you wherever you go, whatever you do."

Aaron felt a deeper love than ever before. It was not a physical love but an affection, a spiritual love. A peaceful feeling from out of this magical attraction that mysteriously binds people together.

"I, too, will love you wherever you are, Amelia." he said. "You will always remain first on the list of happy memories for me, be they of the flesh or in the mind."

***

Throughout the Zakros city-palace, celebration continued long into the night. In the early hours of the morning the tired couple slid under the red and blue blanket in the waiting bed in Amelia's room. They were weary, but Amelia wanted to talk.

"I wanted to tell you this for some time, but I was afraid you would reject me if you knew. I was brought here from Athens as a child slave. My parents were sent to work on the Bull Farm.

178

BOOK 3: Egypt to Crete

That's where I learned about bulls and bull-leaping. I tried it and got pretty good. Then I had a chance to perform at the Bull Court. I was lucky and became known as a bull-leaper. The reason I had to leave the pottery shop was because my master at the farm scheduled me to perform at the festival of *Britomartis*. I had to practice with my team every day at the farm.

"I was given this nice room as a reward for my bull-leaping. My patrons could give me the room, but they could not set me free. Only a decree from a god could do that, they said.

"Now I am no longer a slave, but a priestess. Yet, as a priestess, I am a different kind of slave, a slave to *Britomartis* and the people. How ironic. Freedom is relative to what we think is non-free. No one is ever truly free. There is always someone above you to answer to. Even the Gods have a hierarchy."

"Amelia, can I ask you something?"

"Of course."

"How did you stop that bull?" The question had been on Aaron's mind since the incident.

She snuggled her cheek against Aaron's neck.

"You mean Minos? When I was growing up on the farm Minos was my pet bull. I raised him from a calf. I often fed him lavender. Today I was wearing some lavender-iris oil. He got my scent, thank the gods."

Aaron pulled her close. As she responded the warmth of their

179

touching bodies flamed into passion. Tomorrow, she would start her responsibilities as a Priestess of Zakros, but tonight she would be just a woman in love.

***

The honor bestowed on Aaron lived beyond his life. When Nakht and Captain Sebek saw that it was Aaron who Amelia honored, they were dumb-founded. How could this be? How could this naïve young man become the shinning star, the companion of a master bull leaper in but a few months?

When the details appeared, Nakht, the linguist, would tell this story over the years in a half dozen different languages. In time, stories would be added to stories and grow beyond facts. Amelia and Aaron would become heroes of myths.

***

Before leaving Zakros, Ebu gave Aaron two large pithoi, one full of copper ore and the other cinnabar.

"These are for your labor, Aaron, green and red," he said. "The goddess has looked favorably on you and thus me and our shop."

The pithoi were so heavy that several men with strong ropes were required to get them to and aboard the new ship.

Nakht was greatly impressed with his friend's fortune. Alim, too, he knew would be joyful to see the haul of precious materials.

***

BOOK 3: Egypt to Crete

It took a week for Sebek's crew to disentangle from the Zakros waterfront. Men had made new friends and some had acquired lovers. Leaving such a delightful place was not easy. Two sailors, who had no families in Egypt chose to stay. Sebek's new Cretan crew members, Kar and Romos, would fill the voids. Departure would be after the night of the full moon with the outgoing tide.

For Aaron, his connection with Amelia bade heavily on him. He wanted to stay; yet he wanted to go. Amelia brought him joy and excitement. However, Amelia's new position and fame altered their relationship. No longer could they sneak away to her room and cuddle. She now lived in the upper stories of the city-palace, judging disputes and dispensing charms to the people. Aaron visited her frequently, but duties and attendants subdued the magic of their earlier discovery of each other. Still, they both felt a strong bond of love and even kinship with one another. Perhaps they had been lovers in another lifetime.

As the time of departure approached, Aaron's feelings became jumbled. He knew he must leave, but love has an irrational power.

The desire to return home to Egypt also pulled at him. Proud of his accomplishments, the adventuring son returns a hero. All his friends and neighbors, Ram Da and the pottery workers, would gather around and listen admiringly to his stories. At least that's how Aaron saw it in his mind.

Then again, his feelings for Amelia conflicted with going home. She was so intoxicating Aaron didn't know if he loved her for herself or for the excitement that surrounded her.

And there was still that trace of affection for Nina, his first love, the taker of his virginity. One never forgets the first time, the bonding of physical love.

The lingering thoughts of Nina, Amelia and home weighed heavily on him. What he failed to consider was his responsibility to the Pharaoh and to old Alim. Blinded by the fluctuating moods of too many loves he had forgotten his duties.

***

The sleek wooden ship rocked gently and small waves lapped against the piers in little slurping noises. Aaron and Nakht stood on the dock. Due east, the early morning sun reflected on the Mediterranean waters. On either side of the sparkling line of reflection, the horizon divided the water and sky into two distinct blues and called to the sailors, "Sail on!" Such is the plight of sailors. A new port, a new adventure, the future lies ahead.

Once again it was Nakht who counseled his disoriented friend.

"Aaron, you poor boy. Struck twice already with love's arrow in one trip. Just as there was no future with Nina, there is no future with Priestess Amelia. She is now her people's property. The induction into the priestess' order means she cannot marry. Lovers yes, but marriage no."

BOOK 3: Egypt to Crete

Nakht's directness rung true to Aaron. "I understand, Nakht. It seems love holds as much pain as pleasure."

"Come my friend. Enjoy our new ship. Look. It is a masterpiece. It will be taking us back to the tin in Taurus in style. You get to see Nina again. It's been almost a year. Then back to Cyprus for more copper ingots. Perhaps you'll get struck in the heart with a third arrow there."

Nakht put his arm around his friend and walked him onto the ship. He understood his friend's sadness, his reluctance to leave such a marvelous port and an equally marvelous love. After all, Nakht, too, was a sailor, an adventurer with friends and lovers in many a port. He, too, had experienced the highs and lows of life's constant gifts.

"If all goes well, we'll be back in Egypt in a few months with a haul of ores and ingots–and some great stories that will make old Alim grin." predicted Nakht.

***

Three months later the adventurers arrived in Egypt bringing new materials for Alim to test. More valuable than the earth's materials were the marvelous stories of their trip.

And, indeed, old Alim grinned in satisfaction.

*****

A NOVEL HISTORY OF CLAY

BOOK 3: Egypt to Crete

A NOVEL HISTORY OF CLAY

Bibliography and Notes

EGYPT & CRETE

https://www.metmuseum.org/toah/hd/phar/hd_phar.htm -List of Egyptian pharaohs with dates

http://www.ceramicstoday.com/articles/092501.htm -E. Paste

https://en.wikipedia.org/wiki/Faience -faience overview and details

http://www.ceramicstudies.me.uk/histx104.html -ancient frits and colorants

https://en.wikipedia.org/wiki/Art_of_ancient_Egypt

https://en.wikipedia.org/wiki/Memphis,_Egypt

http://www.ancient.eu/First_Intermediate_Period_of_Egypt/

https://en.wikipedia.org/wiki/Mentuhotep_II

https://en.wikipedia.org/wiki/Thebes,_Egypt

http://www.thekeep.org/~kunoichi/kunoichi/themestream/egypt_alcohol.html#.WOum8CMrI0o

https://en.wikipedia.org/wiki/Flooding_of_the_Nile

https://en.wikipedia.org/wiki/Egyptian_faience

BOOK 3: Egypt to Crete

https://ceramicartsnetwork.org/wp_content/uploads/2010/06/egyptianpaste.pdf -good technical article by Robin Hopper

http://www.cmog.org/article/origins-glassmaking

http://www.makin-metals.com/about/history-of-metals-infographic/

ww.reshafim.org.il/ad/egypt/timelines/topics/music.htm

https://depositsmag.com/2016/07/14/mining-in-ancient-greece-and-rome/

https://en.wikipedia.org/wiki/Prehistoric_Cyprus#Bronze_Age

https://en.wikipedia.org/wiki/Pottery_of_ancient_Cyprus

https://en.wikipedia.org/wiki/Philia_culture

https://en.wikipedia.org/wiki/Mining_industry_of_Cyprus

http://www.metmuseum.org/toah/hd/agbv/hd_agbv.htm -good description of vessels -bronze/clay

http://www.reshafim.org.il/ad/egypt/timelines/topics/bread.htm well written -good

http://www.nytimes.com/1994/01/04/science/enduring-mystery-solved-as-tin-is-found-in-turkey.html?pagewanted=all -tin mines in ancient Turkey

http://www.thekeep.org/~kunoichi/kunoichi/themestream/egypt_soul.html#ka egypt word define

http://penelope.uchicago.edu/Thayer/E/Journals/TAPA/82/Speed

_under_Sail_of_Ancient_Ships*.html

http://www.australianminesatlas.gov.au/education/fact_sheets/tin.html

http://www.ancient.eu/article/999/   -Egypt colors

https://en.wikipedia.org/wiki/Cats_in_ancient_Egypt

http://antiquatedantiquarian.blogspot.com/2015/04/the-minoans-common-people.html   -good photos and supporting literature

https://www.ancient.eu/Minoan_Civilization/

https://ancient-greece.org/art/minoan-art.html

http://ancient-greece.org/history/minoan.html

https://historydaily.org/thats-no-bull-the-minoans-and-their-fascination-with-bovines   -King Minos and bulls

http://www.timemaps.com/civilization/Minoan-civilization

https://en.wikipedia.org/wiki/Murex   -shells to dyes

https://www.youtube.com/watch?v=ev-WeyQjCWk&index=3#t=3951.420204   long history Minoa

http://www.minoancrete.com/zakros.htm   -overview of Zakros

http://www.historywiz.com/minoandiet.html   -foods

https://www.explorecrete.com/archaeology/minoan-herbs.html

http://www.explorecrete.com/crete.html   -brief geography

BOOK 3: Egypt to Crete

http://www.explorecrete.com/history/crete-history.html   -good basic history of period ~2000BC

http://culture-of-peace.info/books/history/crete.html   -slaves

http://www.goldgold.com/gold-in-the-ancient-world.html gold deposits etc.

http://www.minoanatlantis.com/Minoan_Shipbuilding.php wood built

http://www.atlantisbolivia.org/areedboathistory.htm   reed built boats

https://www.youtube.com/watch?v=h2g4F7zZ7uc   -excellent 10min video, goddesses & pots

http://strangehorizons.com/non-fiction/articles/bull-leaping-in-bronze-age-crete/   -Bull-leaping

http://slideplayer.com/slide/4887346/   -transition from Minoan to Mycenaean pottery

https://www.slideshare.net/apetitedelight/mycenean-ppt

https://www.amazon.com/Ash-Glazes-Phil-Rogers/dp/0812237218

https://en.wikipedia.org/wiki/Three-phase_firing -Chemistry, Greek polychrome

https://www.tripsavvy.com/greek-mythology-olympian-gods-and-goddesses-1524431   -GODS

A NOVEL HISTORY OF CLAY

http://arthistoryresources.net/snakegoddess/   -detailed study

http://www.teachinghistory100.org/objects/about_the_object/anc
ient_egyptian_house#:~:text=Egyptian%20homes,were%20free
%20and%20readily%20available.   -good contrast between rich
and poor houses

BOOK 3: Egypt to Crete

Soon to be published:

If you were entertained by this story, I hope you recognized the importance of Egyptian and Minoan influences in the early development of glazes.

Additional books of A NOVEL HISTORY OF CLAY will soon be available. If you'd like to be put on a mailing list to be notified when the next book(s) is out send an email request to *palul.artist@gmail.com.* Any comments can be sent to the same address.

BOOK 4 - *THE OLMECS: American Heads and Jaguars* takes place in Central America where giant stone heads were discovered in 1862. The Olmec culture preceded the Mayan civilization by more than 1500 years and the Aztecs in Mexico by almost 2500 years. Unlike the Egyptians and Minoans, the Olmecs had not yet acquired the potter's wheel or glazes. However, their dynamic and expressive sculptures set the mystical tones for the cultures that followed.

A NOVEL HISTORY OF CLAY

Here's a brief introduction:

BOOK 4: THE OLMECS 1200 - 400 BC
American Heads and Jaguars

As the Minoan Civilization, weakened by a major volcanic eruption, began to be annexed and replaced as the center of European culture by the Aegeans, later to rise as the Greek Civilization, far across the Atlantic in Central America another civilization was evolving.

The patterns were similar: fertile land with a convenient water source for irrigation leading to an excess of crops, peoples migrating into the productive lands causing a population explosion, trading the excess crops for goods resulting in specializations in the building and crafts industries. For order, systems of government developed, usually with a king or high priest at the top.

The unknowns of climate changes and accidents resulted in creating various gods to explain or justify the mysterious acts of nature. To appease and influence the god people were convinced they should support and worship these gods. The silver-tongued and sharp-witted ones in the communities persuaded the slower-thinking people that they, the silver tongues, were the direct messengers of gods

BOOK 3: Egypt to Crete

who could protect the masses from disasters and sufferings. Hence, layers of power created definite levels of statuses: king or priest, government administrators, traders and merchants, builders and craftsmen, farmers and slaves. (The order of importance was not always as listed in the preceding hierarchy. In many societies farmers and builders were considered more important than traders and merchants, etc.)

The Olmec civilization holds its place in history as the first major civilization to occur in the Americas. The Olmecs have been called "the kings of the stone-age," preceding the Maya, Incas, and Aztecs by over a thousand years. Uninfluenced by the earlier civilizations of Europe and Asia, archeologists consider the Olmecs a "pristine" culture, a virgin study.

***

"Stay close to the path," the old trail guard warned, speaking to the long line of people who carried thick woven baskets on their backs making them look bent like hunchbacks. The long line, a thousand strong, trudged steadily up the worn road that wove through jungles and swamps. It was mid-morning.

The guard wore the plumes of an Olmec warrior and carried a short spear along with an obsidian knife in a leather case recovered from a fallen enemy years ago. Also hanging from his leather belt, a mahogany club swung loosely, quickly available to deal with uncooperative workers. The guard's wrinkled face and body wore the scars of time. When a man's usefulness as a fighter ended, the king sent him to the ongoing construction site for the grand pyramid, the tribute to the great god, Kar. The king had told the people that with the offering of such a great pyramid, the god would be certain to watch over and protect the people. It was in their best interest to obey the king and construct this great mound in the middle of the coastal swamp of what is now known as the State of Veracruz, Mexico.

Older warriors, the king had announced, would be honored to serve their remaining years in service to Kar by guarding the long lines of workers as they traveled for hours into the higher hills where they scooped out soil to be carried on their backs down to the construction zone. Day after day, from morning to dusk, thousands of people walked in long lines along trails through the humid jungles, filled their packs with clay soil, returned to the pyramid area, walked up a long ramp, dumped the soil and then repeated the journey.

As the pyramid grew, hundreds of on-site construction workers pounded the soil with the buts of big logs. A layer of adobe mud bricks laid on top held the soil down and created the stepped pyramid shape. Thus far, two steps had been completed. The substructure for the third was three-quarters done with four more layers to go. Eventually a topping of limestone blocks would complete the structure, a monument that would excite archeologists for thousands of years.

A pyramid is more than the sum of its creators. It's more than the sum of construction materials. For humans it points to God. Many cultures have come and gone leaving behind the powerful symbol to represent and connect with their concept of God. Usually, on and within the pyramid are further symbols–suns, stars, eyes, faces, etc.– universal symbols that last beyond time, beyond locations and beyond cultures. Although the Egyptian pyramids are the first ones people think of when the subject comes up, pyramids are found on every continent except Antarctica (maybe they haven't yet been discovered there). Several of the Olmec pyramids and other pyramids in the Americas were actually larger than The Great Pyramid of Egypt. The largest pyramid in the world is in Mexico.

There were two roadways leading into the distant hills, one of people going up with empty containers and the other of people coming down with full ones. On a clear day a person might make four trips up and back. If one looked down from the clouds, the lines of thousands of people would look like ants going to a discovered food source and returning to the nest with little morsels.

The soil contained small volcanic stones mixed in with loam and clay. Occasionally a pure clay deposit would appear, wherein the workers were instructed to deliver baskets of dry clay to the potter's district. Axora liked the clay district. It sat further away on the far side of the pyramid structure. The multitude of forms, the creative activity and burning beehive kilns intrigued the girl, so much so that she always volunteered to make the journey whenever new clean clay was discovered.

Before technology, how many great things have been built by the muscles of massive numbers of men and women (and children) organized to work? The Egyptian pyramids and the Great Wall of China are examples of amazing engineering feats by men organized like ant colonies.

Although the threat of attacks by distant tribes was slim, the greater threat was that of jungle animals, the most fearsome being the jaguar. Jaguars are the third largest of cats in the world behind tigers and lions. Jaguars prefer to hunt at night but reports of day killings were not uncommon. They have been known to attack and kill two cows at once. Dropping from a tree in ambush onto one, a quick bite and twist would snap the neck of the first cow and before the next cow could escape the jaguar would, with a quick bounce and swipe of its wicked claws, disable the second and it's life too would end. The jaguar would then carry off its prey, often times as heavy as the cat itself, up into a tree or to a secluded place to dine.

This apex predator brought both fear and respect to the Olmec peoples. Hence, aside from keeping the "lazy" workers moving, guards were needed to allay the fears of the workers, keeping the lines constantly moving.

Axora, now 12, had been on the line for six years. There was no distinction, other than smaller backpacks, between adults and children. At an early age most small children, unless the son or daughter of a shaman, priest or a noble, was ordered to do the king's bidding. Most either farmed from morning to night or carried the pyramid earth from morning to night. The majority of people accepted their lot, others rebelled and were eliminated in public executions by clubbing which obviously sent a fearful message to the rest.

The builders and craftsmen, because of their special skills, maintained a status between the workers and the upper classes of nobles, priests and shamans. Most of these positions were passed on through family connections, becoming apprentices who, if gifted and motivated, worked their way up into the status of "masters." The king and nobles depended upon the skills of the assorted trades to create the pleasureful marvels of architecture and worldly arts so much desired and appreciated by their classes. Thus, these craftsmen, these artists, were given special respect and treatment.

Axora fell into the worker class (which was the equivalent of a slave class). Axora's six years of hard work created a strong and muscular young girl. By the time the black hairs of puberty appeared around her groin and her breasts budded in little mounds, she had often carried four loads of soil in a day.

Kain, a boy several years older, had watched Axora grow as he carried his loads in the mindless parade of ant workers. He positioned himself a few bodies behind Axora where he could admire the curves of her developing buttocks as they moved in rhythm to her steps. They kept his mind off the boredom. Kain soon lusted after the young adolescent and fantasied and began to plan how to have her.

One afternoon Axora signaled to the guard that she had to pee. The guard motioned to her, pointing into the nearby jungle.

"Do not go too far off the trail," he warned. "Jaguars have been sighted in this area." He moved ahead encouraging the old people and young children in the ant line to keep up the steady pace.

Kain watched Axora leave the line and head into a thicket of trees and vines. Motioning to the man behind him, he said, "I gotta go." The man nodded and Kain slipped into the jungle moving through the trees and reeds in the direction he had seen Axora go.

At the base of a large banyan tree growing in the dark soil at the edge of a thick bamboo grove, Axora lifted her skirt to do her business. The flow of urine felt relieving as her bladder shrunk. *The jungle is awfully quiet,* she thought. She turned to go and there before her stood Kain.

"Leave your skirt up," he commanded to the young girl. She saw a single-minded look of desire on his rough face. His loincloth bulged abnormally. Having heard stories about sexual encounters from the older girls, Axora read his intention. This was not how she wanted it to happen. Certainly not with this

BOOK 3: Egypt to Crete

bad-mannered boy.

Axora backed up to the tree. The smooth gray bark pushed cooly against her back blocking further retreat. Kain moved forward untying his loincloth and grabbed her arm. He pushed her hard against the tree. Holding her arm tightly Kain tried to grab her other arm to pin her up against the tree where he could force his stocky body against her. Before he could catch her free arm, Axora swung her hand into his face and jabbed a finger into his eye.

"Ow!" he screamed, releasing his grip on her other arm.

Axora spun loose and quickly circled behind the tree with Kain angry and swearing right behind her. His wild look and anger terrified her. Kain was two steps away from grabbing her when suddenly a large flash of yellow, black and white landed from above directly on Kain. Before he could scream there was a loud crunch as the jaguar bit through his skull. Axora witnessed the drooling, bloody mouth and teeth clamping into the boy's head. Bits of Kain's brain dripped out between its long teeth and it turned toward Axora. Kain's body twitched and spasmed. She screamed and fled toward the bamboo thicket. The jaguar not wanting to loose what he considered easy prey, released Kain's dead body and made for Axora.

The bamboo trees grew three inches in diameter and close together, so close there was barely room for Axora to squeeze between. Like giant vertical bars the bamboo grew so densely

199

that the jaguar could not penetrate. However, the jaguar quickly reached in with his paw, claws extended, to extract his victim. Just as she squeezed through another pair of bamboo bars the big cat's claws racked her back from her shoulder to her waist. She felt an instant of burning pain and the warmth of wet blood. However, the pain immediately vanished from the pumping adrenalin of terror. With angry snarls the frustrated cat pawed uselessly between the bars of bamboo at the escaping girl....

End of sample of BOOK 4.

BOOK 3: Egypt to Crete

Books by PALUL
(These books can be found on Amazon.com)

Clay Hand-Building And Beyond

Raku And Beyond

3000 Quotes: A Compilation by Palul

Vision-Quest: A Saga of the 1960s - an autobiography

Pollen Grains - A book of poems

Poems of Consequences - Poems

A Novel History of Clay, BOOK 1: The Prehistoric World of Clay

A Novel History of Clay, BOOK 2: Mesopotamia - A Clay Civilization

A Novel History of Clay, BOOK 3: Egypt to Crete - The Pursuit of Glazes

A NOVEL HISTORY OF CLAY

Future books and discoveries in the series:

A NOVEL HISTORY OF CLAY

BOOK 4 - The Olmecs - American Heads and Jaguars

BOOK 5 - Terracotta Warriors - 8000 Full-size Clay Warriors

BOOK 6- Greece and Rome - The Antique Store

BOOK 7 - Han Dynasty

BOOK 8 - Anasazi

BOOK 9 - T'ang Dynasty

BOOK 10 - Sung Dynasty

BOOK 11 - Islamic Luster Glazes

…. on to temporary times.

About the Author

When he reached his sixties Paul Rideout changed his name to Palul because he constantly miss-typed "Paul." It kept coming out with an L in the middle as "Palul."

He says, "It seemed to fit me–an artist name–so I became Palul."

He graduated from the University of Rhode Island in 1962 with a Bachelor of Science Degree in Zoology/Chemistry. Over the years he has worked in eight different labs from Boston to Hawaii as both a research scientist and as a clinical medical technologist.

In 1963-4 he studied art at Massachusetts School of Fine Arts close to the Boston Museum of Art where he spent much of his time "just wandering, visiting the great works of Van Gogh, Cezanne and Gauguin."

When he was thirty (1970) he discovered ceramics.

He says: "I was hooked and could not get enough. I kept work-ing in the lab but my focus turned to clay. In ten years I became an adjunct ceramics instructor for Shasta College in Redding, California. For me ceramics blended art and science in the most perfect way. The subjectivity of art kept me well-balanced with the objectivity of science. I guess I'm a fairly even right-brain, left-brain person."

Considered a master ceramic artist, his art has been shown in numerous galleries and is collected nationally and internationally.

Along with several other books on ceramics, he has published a unique autobiography: *VisionQuest, A Saga of the 1960s.*

For photos of his ceramic work and blurbs on his other books visit his website at *Palul.com.*

BOOK 3: Egypt to Crete

Printed in Great Britain
by Amazon

60138311R00119